SKINSWAPS

■ □ ■ □ ■

ANDREJ BLATNIK

SKINSWAPS

Translated from the Slovenian by Tamara Soban

NORTHWESTERN UNIVERSITY PRESS

EVANSTON, ILLINOIS

Northwestern University Press
Evanston, Illinois 60208-4210

Originally published in Slovenian in 1990 under the title *Menjave kož.*
Copyright © 1990 by Andrej Blatnik. English translation copyright
© 1998 by Northwestern University Press. Published 1998 by
arrangement with Andrej Blatnik. All rights reserved.

Printed in the United States of America

ISBN 0-8101-1656-1 (cloth)
ISBN 0-8101-1657-X (paper)

Library of Congress Cataloging-in-Publication Data

Blatnik, Andrej.
    [Menjave kož. English]
    Skinswaps / Andrej Blatnik ; translated from the Slovenian by
Tamara Soban.
        p. cm. — (Writings from an unbound Europe)
    ISBN 0-8101-1656-1 (hard : alk. paper). — ISBN 0-8101-1657-X
(pbk. : alk. paper)
    1. Blatnik, Andrej—Translations into English. I. Soban, Tamara. II.
Title. III. Series.
PG1919.12.L38M4613 1998
891.8'435—dc21   98-34133
                                                                                CIP

The paper used in this publication meets the minimum requirements
of the American National Standard for Information Sciences—Perma-
nence of Paper for Printed Library Materials, ANSI z39.48-1984.

Kje je koža? Kam ste dali kožo?
    Laibach, *Koža* (Skin)

I've got you under my skin
where the rain can't get in
and where the sweat pours out
    The The, *Uncertain Smile*

sit there with your clothes off
while I look at you. we'll never change.
the world's getting smaller with every
second we breathe.
    Skin, *Breathing Water*

La pelle . . . la unica bandiera . . .
    Curzio Malaparte, *La pelle*

■ □ ■ □ ■

CONTENTS

■ □ ■ □ ■

ACKNOWLEDGMENTS

"Temporary Residence" first appeared in *Whelks Walk Review* 1 (1998); "The Drummer's Strike" first appeared in *Dominion Review* 14 (1996); "The Taste of Blood" and "Rai" first appeared in *Other Voices* 23 (Fall/Winter 1995); "Two" first appeared in *100 Words on the Body,* Iowa City 1993; "Isaac," "The Day Tito Died," "Kyoto," "Billie Holiday," and "Actually" first appeared in *The Day Tito Died* (London: Forest Books, 1993). "His Mother's Voice" is forthcoming in *TriQuarterly.*

Skinswaps

■ □ ■ □ ■

THE DRUMMER'S STRIKE

As THE STICK APPROACHES THE DRUMHEAD, EVERYTHING seems to be lost; look, the saxophone player inhales too early and he's going to blow at the wrong time, the man on the bass acts as though the instrument in his hands has suddenly turned into a dried stick, the trumpet player's eyes are bulging and he's thinking about the red sports car that almost ran him over when he was three years old and had suddenly broken free from his mother and dashed out onto the road, the pianist glances from one end of the keyboard to the other, it seems as if the keys have somehow curved, bent inward, as though the devil had ignited a fire under them, and the singer is also losing control, her garter is slipping, she knows she can only groan inaudibly into the microphone, that is, if she could reach it, because it looks like it will topple any second now, people will drop cutlery onto unfinished meals any time now and desperately start searching for the waiter, the maître d' will hold his head in despair, true, the man in the reception will shrewdly shake his head at the disaster, no, I'm afraid we're all sold out for tonight, but everything is in vain, a good business will go belly up; luckily, the drummer slows down his strike in the nick of time, the stick gently comes to rest on the vellum, and they all start playing right, and the singer caresses the microphone and sings as sweetly as a lark, all is won, the guests clatter their cutlery contentedly, could you save us a table for tomorrow as well, please, they whisper to the maître d', this music is so nice, we'll come, we'll come again.

■ □ ■ □ ■

HIS MOTHER'S VOICE

IN THE CINEMA THE KID WAS WATCHING A HORROR movie. People were screaming in terror. On the screen, an invisible killer was killing off, one by one, the members of a family living in a lonely spot—a house on the outskirts of town. They had not done anything, or if they had, it was not clear what it was; he was killing them, as it were, because it was their fate. All the murders happened in more or less the same way; each time a member of the family would unsuspectingly enter a room where the killer was waiting in ambush for him or her, and the killer would slaughter them. Each time the audience would groan: how could they be so stupid! They should have known there was a killer in the house, and yet they were not at all careful. Not even the soft, harmonious whisper that was heard whenever the killer was close meant anything to them, although it was loaded with significance.

The most horrible scene of all was where the killer called to the little son of the family, who had suspected that something was wrong and was determined to act with utmost caution. He did it by imitating his mother's voice. The little boy naïvely believed that it really was his mother calling him, while in reality she was lying in a pool of blood on the floor, at the killer's feet. Somebody sitting next to the kid whispered: "Be careful, watch out, it's not your mommy, it's not your mommy." At the peak of suspense a woman cried out: "Run!" The little boy did not hear her and did not run away. He went straight to the killer. Everything was clear.

The kid drew in his lips and stared at the screen. He kept repeating to himself that it was just a movie. The killer cut the child to pieces before the little boy could realize that he had made a wrong move, that it had not been his mother. The people felt somehow relieved that it was all over. They had known all along that the little boy would not make it, he was too gullible, it could not have ended any differently, they told themselves. The kid thought: how could he have been so careless and not have recognized the voice? If he had recognized it, he might have been able to defend himself. If only he hadn't let himself be drawn to that room!

Soon afterward the killer was identified and the movie was over. The lights went on in the cinema. People were getting up from their seats and straightening their clothes. Each one hesitated somewhat at the exit, as if unwilling to go out, and then went off into the darkness. The kid was among the last to leave. It was the first time his mother had let him go to the late show, and he was scared. He had a long way to go home, as they lived on the outskirts of town, in a lonely spot, and because of the energy-saving cuts the electricity was turned off at ten, so the streets were not lit. In every bush the kid thought he could see the killer, and while walking he listened intently to every sound, as he could not see anything. Once he suddenly heard something behind him that strongly resembled the whisper that betrayed the killer's presence, but when he turned around it was only a rat running from one sewer to another.

After a few terror-filled minutes he came home. At first he was almost relieved, thinking that he was safe now and he could tell his mother about how he had been so afraid; the fear would then disappear and they would laugh at it together, as they had many times before. But the house was dark, no lights anywhere. Something seemed wrong. Cautiously, he opened the door. He entered the hall. He waited. He did not know what to do. The house was quiet, almost too quiet. Something's wrong, thought the kid. Something was in there. Something . . . What if something happened to mommy? They lived in a lonely part of town, anything was possible. If only he had something that would help if . . . He groped behind the door. He felt something cold under his fingers. He recognized the thing, it was the ax. Yesterday they were chopping wood for the winter with mommy. Mommy praised how strong he had become, since he could split a log in two by himself.

When he took hold of the ax he overturned something and it made a muffled noise. He heard his heartbeat pounding in his ears. He held his breath and waited. The thing inside, in the house, also waited. Then he heard it call out: "Is that you? Kid, is that you?" His first impulse was to drop the ax and enter, then he stopped. It occurred to him that it might not be his mother's voice, although it was similar to it. Very similar. He grasped the handle of the ax firmly. He held it with both hands. Caution. He had to be cautious. Not risk anything. "Kid?" Now the voice seemed even stranger. This was supposed to be his mommy? You're not going to get me, he thought. You're not going to get me.

"Kid, come on in." I'm not going, thought the kid. And I'm not going to run away either. I'll get revenge. You in there, what did you do to her? It's true she let them put me in a special school, so that my schoolmates from the old school don't like me anymore, but all the same, she was my mommy, and tonight she let me go to the late show, although it wasn't a movie for children. I'll get revenge. "Kid?" He was perplexed. He did not know what to do. The voice was very similar to his mother's. More than the one in the movie. How childish that boy in the movie was, he thought. No wonder he caught it. He wasn't cautious enough. "Kid? Answer me!" Now the voice was closer. He realized it was coming into the hall. He gathered his strength and lifted the ax above his head. "Are you here? What's the matter?"

By now his eyes had adjusted to the dark. He squeezed himself into the corner behind the door and waited. He imagined his mommy lying on the floor in a pool of blood, and tears came to his eyes. The whisper that betrayed the killer droned in his ears. Here it goes, he thought. The killer's outline was already visible at the door. The kid whimpered in fear and the figure on the doorstep slowly turned toward him. Through the tears and the dark he could see that the killer did not only copy her voice, but also his mother's appearance. The resemblance was amazing. For a moment he faltered. At that moment the killer in the disguise of his mother caught sight of the ax in his hands, and in spite of the dark, the kid could see how it made the killer's eyes widen and the whites stand out. The ax in his uplifted hands trembled and his doubt reached its peak. Then the killer in the guise of his mother screamed in a dreadful way. The scream was like nothing the kid had ever heard before, least of all the warm, kind voice of his mommy. He felt relieved. Now he knew.

■ □ ■ □ ■

ISAAC

FOR DAYS ON END THEY WERE BEING DRIVEN IN SEALED boxcars, where night had no end. At first they tried to guess what was waiting for them at the end of the journey, later they just prayed. Nobody complained about hunger and thirst any longer, they had all come to terms with everything, only Isaac crouched in a corner and persistently worked away at the hardwood floor with his fingernails. The hours went by and he felt his fingers turning into raw, shapeless lumps. When he looked around at his fellow passengers, he saw that their faces were transfigured, already contemplating the next world. He knew that in their present state they could no longer understand his plan. He had to do it on his own. When he was on the point of thinking that his strength had run out and that he would join them in prayer, light seeped through a crack in the floor.

Then the hole widened quickly. Soon it was big enough for him to see through to the crossties rushing by. Then it was so wide that he knew they could squeeze themselves through it, after all the starving they had gone through in the wooden cage. He nudged the man sitting next to him. "Let's go," he said. "We can go." The man looked at him, bewildered, and when Isaac saw his eyes in the daylight coming through the scratched-out floor, he felt almost sorry for disturbing him. "Pray," the man whispered kindly. "Pray."

He stretched his arm as if to put it around Isaac's shoulders. Isaac drew away from him, and the man's arm dropped limp by his side. "I'm going," Isaac said out loud. "Here's a way out." "Pray." The quiet murmur was all around him, although nobody had lifted their head. "Pray."

They've gone crazy with the suffering, he thought. Prayer won't save them. They're going to die. Die. Then it occurred to him that they might not be praying for salvation after all, that they might be just trying to prepare themselves for the inescapable, but there was not much difference between the two explanations to him. He squeezed himself through the opening. He touched the ground feet first and the crossties struck his heels; the dull thumps felt good, they made him aware that he was not just running away in a dream. Then he let go. It did not hurt him at all, he only felt the blood ooze from the scratches. He lay on his back, stretched completely flat, and watched the underframes and wheels race by. The train was a long one, and many a car had passed over him when he suddenly realized in horror that it was slowing down. It was true; the train was coming to a stop. Then there were no cars left and he was blinded by daylight. Behind him, he heard the screeching of the brakes. When he regained his eyesight the first and only thing he saw was a highly polished army boot. He looked up. The officer was unbuckling his holster. "We've arrived. Were you leaving us?" he inquired, smiling. Isaac tried to jump up, to run away, but all his strength had deserted him. His limbs filled with air, and then suddenly his memory was flooded by his entire life, by the endless journey, and his hands started to hurt terribly. "Animal," he breathed hard, "animal." For a moment he wondered what he had meant by that—they had been driven like animals, he would die like an animal, and, actually, he had also lived like an animal, without respect for the faith of his fore-fathers—but he realized that this kind of thinking was now irrelevant and trivial. The officer bent toward him; Isaac could see the well-oiled gun glitter in the sunlight. "I may be an animal," he said, "but this animal is philo-sophical. If you can't change the fate of the majority, you have to share it." He aimed his gun at Isaac's head and Isaac wondered: will I feel anything at all? Then, in the split second he had remaining, he realized that beyond the barrel of the gun awaiting there was Shekinah.

■ □ ■ □ ■

THE DAY TITO DIED

IT WAS A SUNDAY, QUITE WARM, IN THE AFTERNOON WE
had been playing Frisbee in the street. Then I went in and
sat down in front of the TV, and as soon as I heard the
music they were playing I knew. I was alone at home,
waiting for my mother and father to come home, and in
my uneasiness I went to the kitchen and cut myself a slice
of bread, I chewed it slowly, the primeval monotonous
rhythm of my jaws somehow pacified me. When my
mother and father arrived I was just munching the last
bite. We sat down at the table and didn't talk, at about ten
o'clock in the evening the telephone rang, they were calling me to come to school, and I didn't know what would
happen next, my mother and father didn't know either, I
put on clean pants and my best shoes and went to school.
Some of my teachers and fellow students were there, at
first they looked at me strangely, then they said they'd
called me because they thought it might be necessary to
prepare a commemoration and I was good at those things,
but now they'd changed their minds, there would be no
commemoration and I could go home. I went home, there
was no one in the streets, and at home I got together a few
books of partisan and revolutionary poetry in case they
still wanted a commemoration the following day, then I
lay down on my bed and stared at the ceiling. Only about

a year later I learned that right after I'd left home my mother called the school and told them I was ill and they were to leave me alone whatever it was they were doing. That's why they invented the commemoration, sent me home and did whatever it was they were doing without me; what it was I still don't know to this day.

■ □ ■ □ ■

T W O

As I lie in the twilight of my room, I can feel the animal lick my hand hanging over the side of the bed, like a silkworm, a withered coil. The animal's eyes glitter feverishly, and when its rough tongue flickers over my dry skin, sparks spray. Because I can't name the animal, I think: I've thought up this animal. I *believe* I've thought it up, but this brings no solution. The animal is quietly breathing beside my bed, content, and through its breathing it is letting me know: yes, that's right. You've thought me up. You did it well, down to the last detail, to my sharp teeth, to the hunger piercing me. Please, go on thinking me up, otherwise I won't be able to spring upon you and bite your throat once the hunger becomes unbearable.

I feel that I should stop thinking about it, perhaps I really have thought it up, perhaps it isn't real. Like this room, which *seems* like a room, while actually I am, I know, in the womb of a body I don't know. But, as usual, the worst possibility is that all contrast is but a mirror reflection of sameness: what if the animal is thinking me up too? Then we'll both be finished, no matter who starts first. That is why I lie in a room that is not a room, and the animal, anxious with hunger, licks my hand.

■ □ ■ □ ■

APOLOGIA

So what, says He, who's there to judge me for the error?

■ □ ■ □ ■

KYOTO

"Tea-drinking," said Jay, "is a skill that takes years to learn, if not decades."

We looked at each other. We had taken these words rather well, we felt. Nobody had screamed. We were holding our china cups tightly in our palms. Then we heard a polite cough from the back of the room. We turned around, though we need not have.

Of course, it was Sam, who else could it have been.

"Excuse me," he started unctuously, "did you say ... years?"

"Years," nodded Jay seriously. "If not decades."

"But," Sam smiled somewhat uncertainly, "I'm staying in Kyoto only for another week or so. No, even less. Actually, five days."

Well, in that case you will never know how to drink tea, we thought.

"In that case the art of drinking tea will probably stay unknown to you forever," Jay said obligingly.

Now he will say: But..., we thought.

"But...," said Sam with disapproval.

But what? we thought. What in the world, 'but'? Everything is clear.

"Yes, I am listening to you," Jay said kindly. "Is anything the matter?"

He will object, saying that he came to Kyoto with the sole purpose of learning how to drink tea.

"I came to Kyoto with the sole purpose of learning how to drink tea," objected Sam.

Jerk! we thought. So you came in vain.

"I can understand your point of view," said Jay. "In this case, I am afraid your decision to come to Kyoto might not have been the right one."

Now he will want him to explain it in detail, we were horrified, now he will begin with: Are you saying . . .

"Are you saying," began Sam, "that my coming here was completely useless? In your brochure it was written that the mystery of tea was accessible to everyone who came to your school. And that's why I came to Kyoto, after all. What I'm saying is: I am here, I had to pay for the trip, I have to pay for my hotel room, I even had to pay for coming to your school, and now . . ."

So you threw your money away, probably not for the first time, nor the last either! we thought.

Jay smiled. "Some people say," he said, "that the point of money is to spend it."

"Yes, yes," Sam refused to be distracted, "but the ways are different, you'll have to admit that much, different. I could have given my money to the poor . . ." He paused dramatically.

"People do that, true," remarked Jay, "and it is probably not the worst of possibilities at our disposal."

". . . or I could have invested it in some company that would then fail . . ."

Stop, stop, we thought. You are being a nuisance. Go away, this thing is simply not for you. Why should our teacher concern himself with you when you do not want to learn? Let him take interest in us. But he is so patient, he will let you go on nagging him . . .

"You might have regretted that," inferred Jay sympathetically.

"No more than I regret my coming to Kyoto. You must understand me, I really can't dedicate years and decades to such a simple thing as drinking tea." Sam was resolute.

"A simple thing? Did you say a simple thing?" said Jay with amazement.

"Of course. Let's be realistic: any child can drink tea."

"Good Lord! Just the preparation of tea according to the rules of our school takes four hours and requires hundreds of precise and elaborate gestures that take years to learn! And drinking comes only after that!"

"And where does this very special way of drinking get you?" asked Sam.

Now, at last, Jay will scratch his eyes out, we said to ourselves. Otherwise, we will be forced to do it ourselves. After all, now he is wasting our time, our money, our admission fee.

"I am holding a cup of tea in my hands," began Jay. "In its green color I can see all nature. When I close my eyes, I discover green hills and pure water in my heart. When in silence, alone with myself, I sit and drink tea, I feel how it is all becoming a part of me. And when I share this cup of tea with others, they also become one, with me and with nature . . ."

Don't interrupt him, we thought, just don't interrupt . . .

"This," interrupted Sam, "is utter mumbo jumbo. And a little pathetic at that. Cheap Oriental mystique, actually quasi-mystique."

Jay observed him silently for a long time, and we started glancing toward the door. Yes, it was time to leave, we thought. And not only for Sam. After all, we did get something for our money—a few nice words and a cup of tea, if that thickish bitter liquid is to be called that. We did as we had been told: you put your cup into your right palm, turn it twice clockwise, finish the tea in three swallows, again turn the cup twice in the opposite direction . . . and that's that, as far as the first lesson is concerned.

"I am not an Oriental, sir," Jay finally said. "I am an American, like you."

That is right, we thought. He is American. We said to ourselves: this could be a turnabout. We waited to see what would happen next. Anything was possible now, and especially sentences like: Then you of all people should know that the ratio between the capital invested and value created should be in your favor! Or perhaps: This doesn't absolve you in the critical eye of history! Or even: Traitor! You betrayed your people!

"If you're American," said Sam smugly, pleased with himself, as if he had finally achieved what he had been wanting to all along, "you won't reject my proposal."

For the first time now, Jay was slightly perplexed. "What do you propose?" he asked cautiously.

"A small bet. If you win, I'll immediately write out a check for one hundred thousand dollars to your school. I'll take out my checkbook right away."

We all drew in our breath. So did Jay. One hundred thousand! Like hell! Only last night he let us pay for his beer!

"Money does not mean much to us teachers of tea," Jay replied uncertainly.

"Oh, well, in that case forget about my proposal," Sam shrugged ingenuously, and the lurking way he was observing Jay did not escape our notice.

"And what if you should win the bet?" the question almost eluded Jay's control.

"Well, in that case you'll come with me, back to America."

"I do not want to go to America," Jay was surprised. "I cannot live without tea anymore."

"You won't be without tea in America," said Sam. "I'll open a school of tea. Americans won't have to go to

Kyoto anymore to get the proper education, and the whole business will be cheaper in America, due to travel expenses, among other things."

"But we already have schools of tea in America," said Jay cautiously. "One in New York, one in Seattle, and one in Honolulu."

So, we thought, Sam could not make much profit on this thing. Of course he could not be competitive with his total lack of understanding of the essence of tea. He will really go back empty-handed from his trip, poor guy.

"That's good," said Sam soberly. "It shows that it can also work in America. The only thing left for me to do is establish our school better than your branch schools. And this shouldn't be too complicated. We'll promote our firm as a genuine American school of tea-drinking and not as a branch of a Japanese firm."

We could not help rolling our eyes at the things he said. Who for heaven's sake drinks tea in America, let alone teaches others how to do it? It was clear to everyone, except obviously to Sam, that you cannot sell the art of tea-drinking unless you play upon Eastern exotica.

Jay refused to be drawn. He said warily: "If I am not mistaken, you mentioned a sort of bet."

"Yes, a bet," said Sam. "Are you interested?"

It's obvious, we thought, it's too obvious.

"Well, in a way," Jay said, apparently without much interest.

It was clear. He was interested. He was very interested.

"The thing is very simple," said Sam. "You claimed before that thanks to the tea skills you had become one with nature. It's just a matter of proving this."

We waited. Sam waited. Jay waited.

"The thing is," continued Sam, "last night, for instance, I was going back to my hotel late at night. I was walking in a deserted district, I could see the eyes of wild animals glittering in the dark, I could hear terrifying snarls . . ."

We listened in amazement. What is he talking about? We were all staying together, in the Grand Hotel, two hundred meters from the railroad station, and the highway ran beside it. What eyes of wild animals, what snarling? Japan is so densely populated you can walk for days on end without finding a spot you could not see a neon sign from. And he says: a deserted district.

Jay listened silently. Perhaps he never goes out of this little bamboo room, we thought, and he does not know what the world is like outside. But it would have been enough for him to look at the city map to see there were no thickets like the one Sam was describing anywhere, let alone one with a hotel for Americans in it.

". . . and so it occurred to me that, for thousands of years, people have actually been inventing all sorts of implements to subjugate nature somehow, while at the same time they've failed to understand it completely, they don't see its quintessence, they only see its deceptive forms of appearance . . ."

We looked at Jay; he was nodding thoughtfully. A simpleminded person would have said that he had taken the bait.

". . . and therefore they'll never know how to become one with it. They'll always remain strangers in the world, doomed to endless struggle without hope of success . . ."

We exchanged meaningful glances. What philosophy! It made us feel as if we were sitting at home in front of the TV and watching commercials.

". . . and the only possibility they have of not being defeated in this struggle is to become reconciled with the fact that they had actually lost it at the time when they separated from nature, when man became a super-species. But it's precisely because they are a super-species that they cannot become reconciled with it."

Undoubtedly Jay chewed well on the bait. To him Sam's words probably exuded the aroma of koans, of

Mumonkan, and he was attracted to such fragrances. He became impatient. He said: "Yes, yes, certainly . . . And what would the bet be?"

Now, we knew, the letdown must follow. It must become apparent that this bet is actually nothing special . . . "Actually, it's nothing special," said Sam coaxingly. "It's simply that . . ."

If he said "simply," this is going to be a long story, we thought wearily.

"Last night, for instance, our hotel shook. Nothing unusual, nothing unexpected. An earthquake. A very frequent thing in these parts. Tectonic agitations. In short, an everyday occurrence. Well, you know the way it is. In our hotel, we Americans are mixed with the Japanese. And not just us. What I'm trying to say is that the hotel has a racially mixed clientele. And when yesterday's earthquake happened, it became apparent that what was at issue here was more than just the color of the skin. All the whites came rushing to the hotel lobby, everyone grabbing what they could, we were all in pajamas, thrown out of our sleep . . ."

This time only a few of us exchanged glances, perhaps the ones who had slept soundly all night and, to use a phrase, had not even dreamed of it.

" . . . but only us, the whites, and not a single Asian—or what should I call them. And this really makes one think that there might be, after all, something in this tea link with nature. Maybe people who drink tea really are somehow one with nature . . ."

Well, maybe, we thought, the Japanese have simply gotten so accustomed to such little earthquakes that they simply can not be bothered.

"Not all the Orientals drink tea," Jay ventured.

"But still," Sam persisted, "all the same!"

All the same, what? we wondered. Maybe even Sam could not have answered that.

"And the bet?" asked Jay. It was evident—his calm was crumbling; at a sum that continued to dance in front of everyone's eyes, his calm was disappearing like shaving foam under a razor. The bet, of course, the bet. Now things can not go on without the bet.

"Is it a bet then?" said Sam, now on the lookout with his whole being. "Shall we bet?"

The atmosphere grew electric. Jay undoubtedly felt there was something behind this offer. He must have felt it. It was in the air. We could have touched it—if we had dared to reach out. Jay probed each one of us with his eyes, as if he were trying to find in us, who were supposed to know Sam better than he did, the answer to the question: what lies behind all this? But our eyes were cast downward, although we could have looked him straight in the eye; we did not know what lay behind.

"Well, perhaps I might bet," admitted Jay, increasingly prudently, "but you should tell me first what the bet actually consists of."

"It's simple," hastened Sam, and we were horrified at this word. "If I'm not mistaken you claim that you become one with nature when drinking tea . . ." He paused significantly.

"Yes," confirmed Jay.

"With all living creatures . . ." Another pause.

"Yes," repeated Jay.

"So that you form a harmonious whole with all living beings . . ."

"Yes."

". . . and that nothing natural is alien to you, that nothing living disgusts you . . ."

"Yes."

"Well, in that case," concluded Sam triumphantly, "eat this."

He bent to the ground and reached for something. We all turned to look at him, we all looked down his extended arm, our eyes boring into his closed fist. No, we were not quick enough, we were not as quick as he was. We did not see anything.

Jay dashed toward him. "What? What?" he asked nervously. He no longer tried to hide that he was completely perplexed; perhaps he was aware that he was unable to conceal it. We stepped closer, too; we formed a circle around Jay and Sam. We stretched our necks in curiosity. Sam was clutching his find, which was to decide about one hundred thousand dollars, in his fist. The absurdity of the situation quickened our heartbeat. We were waiting for Jay to tell him to show what he had. "Show me what you have," said Jay.

Sam slowly opened his fist.

On his palm crouched a five-centimeter-long and proportionately fat caterpillar. Automatically we first wondered how he had managed to find such a loathsome thing in the middle of immaculate Japan, and we were at first on the point of accusing him of having brought it with him. Then we had a good look at the animal. It was covered with thick shaggy hair, which made it look all the more repulsive. Besides that, it started to tremble all along its length, as if it felt the weight of our looks upon it. Watching that quivering nasty thing made one's eyes smart.

"Eat this," repeated Sam.

Jay gaped at him, and a sickly bluish pallor gradually covered his face; we could see it descending from his straight-cut hair down to his neck. Of course, it is not an easy task, we thought, but for one hundred thousand dollars, one would swallow hard even after a morsel like this. Besides, the Japanese—as we had learned in the hotel dining room—were used to taking into their mouths a lot of things we could not even bear to look at. It is true that Jay is American, we said to ourselves, but in Japan he probably does not have ham and eggs for breakfast every day, as we who are only visiting here do.

"This?" he asked slowly, very slowly, as if he wanted to give Sam ample time to change his mind. "You can't be serious. This?"

"This," replied Sam.

Jay looked around him uncertainly. We followed his look and saw what he did, what he saw day in and day out, while we had not noticed before, and—immersed in musings about tea skills—might otherwise never have noticed: the cracks in the walls of the tea school, the rush mats frayed at the edges, the stains on the ceiling indicating that the water-resistant paint was giving way. Perhaps if one drinks enough tea one does not notice water dripping on one's head, we thought mischievously.

"Will you take the bet?" asked Sam. We waited. We waited for quite a while. And then, suddenly, Jay turned around and reached into Sam's open hand. In all probability he never closed his mouth from the moment he saw what Sam had picked up from the floor, and now he raised his hand to his mouth, leaving Sam's palm empty. We realized: he was trying to be faster than his second thoughts, faster than disgust. And he succeeded: his hand did not hesitate before his mouth, he withdrew it in the same motion, and swallowed loudly. We saw his Adam's apple bob, and the veins in his neck stand out. Then his eyes bulged and we saw him shudder, close his eyes, and go weak at the knees. We looked at Sam. Now he was pale, paler than Jay had been before. Obviously he had not expected such an outcome, after all, and, regarding the way he let others pay for his drinks, he probably did not enjoy squandering money very much.

It serves you right, we thought spitefully. Now take out your checkbook, you arrogant fool. And write the figure, right to the last zero. We are all witnesses. If only you had to sell every single thing you possess to pay off the debt!

At that moment a frightening groan escaped Jay's lips. He turned on his heels and fell to his knees. During the fall, the contents of his stomach burst out of his mouth, and he left a trail of half-digested food on the wall, oozing slowly toward the floor. Eventually, his body stopped shivering, and only mucus came from his mouth. He wiped his mouth on the sleeve of his blue coat, in the armpit of which we thought we could see sewn-on patches for a moment. The earned money will come in handy for his tea school, we thought. And he can now be considered a sort of hero. He is a hero, too. Which one of us would have done this—for someone else's sake?

"Start writing the check," croaked Jay in a glassy voice. He wanted to lean his hand on the wall, but he placed it exactly on the trail he had left during his fall, and at the touch of something wet he looked up, and the sight of what was directly in front of him made him jerk his hand back, so that his body swayed dangerously and it seemed that he would fall into the middle of his own vomit. But he caught himself. He regained his balance.

We looked at Sam. He looked at us. He could see in our faces the final affirmation of what he already knew: that there was no way out for him. Then he looked at Jay. He gazed at him for a long time, as if spellbound by the painful sight. And suddenly something caught his attention, something wriggling on the floor, in the vomit. He bent down to see better, and when he pulled himself erect again, his face shone with triumph.

"I'm afraid you haven't won the bet after all," he said. "The pest is still here."

We drew near, and, true enough, there in the filth squirmed the caterpillar. It did not appear to have been affected in any way by those few seconds spent in Jay's insides.

Jay—with great effort—also took a look, and as soon as he was convinced of the truth of the matter, he closed his eyes in despair.

"Actually, you lost the bet," continued Sam. "You

have by no means become one with this caterpillar, no, we couldn't say that you have become one with it at all. Or," he turned to us, "would someone wish to claim that, despite everything?"

Against our will, we shook our heads. One thing was clear: none of us would pay for his beer anymore. Not anymore.

"That part about becoming one with nature was meant in a more spiritual sense," said Jay weakly. "To become one also physically, it should become part of me. And for that I would have to murder it."

"That's right," said Sam. "You'd have to murder it, if that's what you call it."

"Murder," said Jay, "murder . . ."

"Don't speak now as if you had some great qualms about it," retorted Sam. "You had no qualms before. You were blinded by the money and didn't think it was murder at all."

Jay blushed scarlet, now in the opposite direction, from his neck up to the crown of his head. Slowly and carefully he was drawing himself erect.

"Yes," he said tiredly. "Yes. I was blinded by the money. Perhaps it really is time for me to return to America. Perhaps I do not belong here, in Japan. Perhaps I never have belonged here."

"What is Japan nowadays but a poor-quality instant copy of America?" asked Sam, aloof. "What else are all these McDonalds, all these slot-machine halls, all these copied metropolitan streets, all this neon and metal?"

"This," said Jay, "is Japan without tea. Japan which does not know how to drink tea anymore. They still drink it, but they do not know how to drink it anymore." He went toward the door. "I am going to pack my luggage. When are we leaving?"

"Let me tell you something," said Sam. "That tea almost made me throw up."

We could kill him, it occurred to us. Tonight we could fill him up with drink—if we paid for the drinks, he would surely get blind drunk—and when he fell asleep, we could break into his room and we could . . .

Jay waved us off with his hand. "Go," he said. "Go. I'll find you at the Grand Hotel. And then we'll go home. Home." Absentmindedly he started to chuckle.

Really, we could kill him, we thought as we were going up the steps to board the bus, while we were riding along the wide avenues of Kyoto, when our slant-eyed guide first asked us how our tea school had been. Lamely, we muttered it had been wonderful, and then she went on to explain all about this or that temple or this or that imperial palace. We could kill him, we thought toward the evening, as the outlines of *Kinkaku-ji,* the Golden Pavilion, were sinking behind us in the twilight, and we were still thinking about it the next day, as we were hauling our luggage to the *shinkansen,* and speeding at 220 kilometers per hour toward Tokyo, toward the Narita airport, toward home, leaving Kyoto and the tea school behind us at an incredible speed. We could kill him, but we will not, because civilized people do not do that out of outrage and disgust, but for more substantial reasons. No, together with him and Jay we will return to our country, live there as we had before, we will try to remember our visit to Japan just by the chemical layers on our slides, and at night we will dream about the green dollar bills, they will appear in front of our eyes, one by one, all the hundred thousand of them, and at that sight there will be a pleasant tingle down our throats, as if we had managed to swallow that caterpillar and keep it down, and, whenever we have a chance, we will talk about how Western man has lost his true bond with nature, and we will travel only to the places where our neighbors have already been and returned without any shocks, and our children will decide to get away from our philistine way of life, from our narrow-minded bourgeois views, and perhaps, on their flight, they will enroll in the very school of tea that Sam is going to open, and it will be Jay who will teach them about tea, the one and the same Jay we saw fall to his knees and throw up because he was disgusted to become one with a part of nature.

■ □ ■ □ ■

THE TASTE OF BLOOD

WET HEATHER COVERED THE FACE OF THE DROWNED GIRL the boys from the village had dragged out of the water and laid by the side of the road. People stood in a silent circle around her, watching drops of water slowly rolling down the stems and dropping on the asphalt, one after another. Like strikes on the death drum, thought Katarina. Thump. Thump. Thump. Thump. Now that she thought about it, the comparison seemed ridiculous, but before, when she had only taken in the sound, it sounded good. Very good.

Finally, the police arrived and tried to do their job. The boy who had tossed his fishing hook in the water and then saw the drowned female body at his feet was answering the questions with a strangely calm, somewhat dejected voice. The pen in the policeman's hand twitched every now and then. Short, routine notes. Name? Residence? Occupation? Time of discovery?

Finally, it occurred to someone to cover the naked body with a dusty blanket taken from the back seat of his car. To reach the blanket he first had to remove a crate of potatoes he was obviously taking God-knows-where. He puffed and strained but was not able to drag the heavy crate out. He asked somebody to help him. The other man muttered something, but helped him anyway.

They put the crate beside the car. It did not escape Katarina's notice how, once the owner headed toward the body with the blanket in his hands, the man he had asked for help quickly reached into the crate, stuffed a few potatoes into his pockets, and, looking around him, sauntered away. Now he's off to cook lunch, she thought, in spite of herself.

Others were obviously more interested in the sight of a naked female body than in their lunch, and there was after all enough logic in that: Katarina contemplated their paunches, the graying stubble on their faces, the mud on their boots, their knotty, gnarled hands, and it seemed to her that in spite of everything they probably had more opportunity to have lunch than to see a naked woman, even if only a dead one. That was why they now shifted their feet, changing the view, trying to find the best one, until the police told them to disperse. This is what they eventually did—some of them quietly muttering, others with complete docility and resignation. The owner of the blanket started to move backward, but the policeman motioned for him to finish what he had started to do. The man hesitated and then slowly let the blanket drop and drape the body. As soon as he had finished, the policeman started waving him away. And so he went. As he pushed the crate back into his small car, the veins on his neck stood out under the strain, but he managed on his own. There was no one left to help him.

Katarina continued to lean against her bicycle until she thought she felt a probing look on her back, and when she turned around to show the intruder that she did care about who was looking at her and how, she realized that it was the policeman; of course, all the other men had gone away long before, and the only other woman there beside herself had her eyes covered with a dusty blanket.

"Aren't you going home, sweetie?" asked the policeman, looking her straight in the eye, kind and, in a way, threatening at the same time. This is the look of a Master, Katarina thought. And so any answer would be wrong. And she remained silent.

"You like watching things like this, don't you?" he asked again, and Katarina could not help noticing how his look grew more intense. More kind, more threatening. Like adding ornaments to the basic melody, she thought. Maybe I should really go home, before the percussion starts.

"Me?" Katarina feigned ignorance, as if there were someone else there at that moment. She remembered the rule that always worked, everywhere: when questioned by a Uniform, you know nothing. And it seemed that it should not be difficult this time: she really knew nothing, except that, when she saw a group of men standing and watching, she stopped to watch.

"You," the policeman sounded final. A strike on a bass drum, recorded next to the drum head.

"Leave me alone, I have to go home," said Katarina and felt the blood rushing to her cheeks. "Home. I'm late as it is."

"Late, late," murmured the policeman, closing his eyes, and it seemed as if his words had taken on another, different meaning. "Late, the late one. Did you know the late one?"

Katarina shook her head.

"I didn't think you did," said the policeman contemplatively. "Before, everybody knew her. Now nobody will want to know about her. That's the way it goes."

What is he talking about? thought Katarina. And asked: "What are you talking about?"

"You're too young for me to start explaining it to you," the policeman sounded somehow benevolent. "You don't know enough . . ." He glanced at the body covered by the blanket, and then immediately looked back at Katarina. Checking, flashed through Katarina's mind. He's checking me out.

She could feel the blood tingling in her cheeks. Listen, old man, she thought, I'm twenty-six. Don't tell me I'm too young. My fellow students from high school have been married for quite a while now. They've got children. Some of them old enough for kindergarten. Listen, old man . . .

Then, like a counterpoint: Don't talk. Shut up. Remain silent, completely silent.

And she remained silent.

"You're quiet? As they say: those that are silent are half-forgiven," said the policeman. "But they can still get convicted for the other half." He ran a hand over his mustache, and in his gesture there was something that reminded Katarina of the man she was trying to forget. No, she thought, oh no, no, no. Don't feel guilty. It's a gesture. It's just a gesture, a superfluous gesture, one of a thousand. People make thousands of gestures. Superfluous ones. Forget him. As if he didn't exist, you hear me?

"You remind me of my father," she said, and the policeman nodded and again smoothed his mustache.

"Who do you belong to?" he said. "Daddy? Mommy? Or someone else? Who comes to give you a kiss on the cheek before you close your eyes at night, baby?"

No, no, thought Katarina. Like Father. Father. Standing in the door of her bedroom. Looking in. Whispering: "I'll be right there to give you a kiss on the cheek, my little Katarina! Right away!" While she was pulling her blanket over her head and chewing her lips. Like Father. The same. The same gesture . . . The same voice. Like Father.

She felt the taste of blood in her mouth.

"What do you want?" she said in a hard, hoarse voice, and when she heard its sound she thought: Filter it. Filter it! Not because you can irritate him. But because with a voice like this, sharp like a chain saw, there is no harmony with the surroundings; the mist over the marshes. The quiet pastoral scene. If the voice were to match the world as it appears here and now, it should sound like a breeze through the reeds.

Of course, she told herself, such a rebuke was out of place—how can a female body covered with a dusty blanket be in harmony with a pastoral scene? And the man stuffing potatoes in his pockets? And this man in uniform, running his hand over his mustache again and again? No, there is no harmony; there cannot be any harmony. Say whatever you want. If you really want to talk.

"Want?" The man was surprised. "Why, I want everything, of course. We all want everything, babe, it's just that some don't say so out loud. Didn't you know?"

What is he talking about? went through Katarina's mind. He's blabbering. Generalizing. Not saying anything you can relate to. Her father. Her father would talk the same way.

"But that's too general," the policeman corrected himself. "We all want everything, but that's beside the point now; you're not interested in that. What you want to know is what I want. What I want from you. You don't care about the rest. Right?"

Katarina nodded. He was right. She did not care; she did not even care about the woman under the blanket. Actually, she had stopped only because there, among the people gathered around the corpse, a murmur was spreading, a murmur that sounded so very similar to the sound she had once searched for but could not find. She lengthened and widened the sinusoid on the generator of sound, but it would not sound right, until she, sick and tired of machines, turned the whole thing off. That was a long time ago, and she was no longer exactly sure what she had needed the sound for, but the moment she heard it again, it seemed somehow vital, somehow . . . inevitable. Yes, inevitable. That was why she had stopped and gotten off her bicycle in the first place. She saw the woman only later.

No, she did not care, since now that the people were gone, the sound that had stopped her was also gone, and she knew that what she was still hearing in her ears was just an illusion. When she sat down in front of her machines, it would no longer be there. And mathematics would not be able to bring it back. It was lost.

"Actually, what I'd really want," said the policeman, "is, in a way, the same thing as everyone. Yes, now that I come to think about it, I'm actually the same as everyone. Yeah." He gazed at Katarina with a tragic expression on his face, "Isn't that awful?"

"Everything?" asked Katarina.

"Everything . . . and above all that. You know what."

No, she did not know.

The policeman made a pointed gesture with his hand. "You know . . . it. What else? That's what it's all about. Always."

Katarina blushed.

"Don't blush," said the policeman, "It's not a bad thing. We've both done it a thousand times, what's the use of pretending. If not in reality, then at least in our thoughts. And some people say it's even better in your imagination."

Yes, Katarina remembered uneasily, that's exactly the way Father talked when he came back from prison. Lost in his thoughts, he would suddenly begin to laugh, and when somebody asked him why he was laughing, he'd say: "It's even better in your imagination . . . You wouldn't believe it, but it's even better in your imagination." And he would laugh even harder.

"You remind me of my father," she said.

"If I remind you of your father," said the policeman with deliberation, "and if this memory is as unpleasant as

I can see by your expression, why don't you spit on me then?"

"You're wearing a uniform," said Katarina automatically and blushed.

"So what?" asked the policeman. "I've got skin underneath it, like everyone else. And maybe that's what all this is about. The skin. What you'd spit on, what brings back memories, are not the clothes. And that I can't take off."

That's true, thought Katarina, he's right.

"I," said the policeman, "I'm not your father. I'm not. You know that."

You're not, thought Katarina. But you're like him. Just like him.

"And what would you say," he continued, "if I told you to come with me?"

A shiver ran through Katarina.

"I had nothing to do with her," she said numbly.

The policeman smiled.

"I wasn't going to arrest you. You're not guilty, I know that. It's not my uniform calling you, it's"—here he paused and winked at her—"my skin."

"I don't understand," said Katarina.

"Well, it's simple. I can take you . . . Where do you want to go? My place?"

"I have to go home," said Katarina.

"Home," said the policeman under his breath. "OK, home." He motioned to his partner. "I'll be going now," he said. "Wait for the hearse. You can ride back with it."

His partner, a young boy, pouted in disappointment.

"Together with a dead woman," he said. "With a woman like this." And he looked at Katarina.

"You know how it is," said the policeman cheerfully. "My turn, your turn. You can make it up to me."

"Yeah, yeah, I will," said the other one without taking his eyes off Katarina. "You remind me," he said to her, "of my sister. I could be your brother."

"Too late," said the older one, "too late. I already remind her of her father. Another time."

"U-huh," said the boy and disappointedly spit next to the drowned woman's head. "I shouldn't have wasted my time earlier."

"Oh, come on! There's plenty of women in this village. You'll manage."

"Their hands smell of dirt," murmured the boy and dried his palms on his trouser legs. "And besides—now their men have gotten on top of them. Now that they've seen this."

He motioned toward the ground and continued to look at Katarina.

"We'd better go," the man with her father's features whispered in her ear. "Sometimes the young one gets impatient . . . He wants more than his share. And then things can get out of hand. Get in the car, come on, hurry up."

Katarina wanted to say that she was not going anywhere, that she was leaving the way she had come, by bicycle, and when she felt like it, but all that remained was: "I've got my bike with me."

"See," called the policeman to the boy, "if you really don't want to ride with the drowned woman, there's something for you here! Why don't you ride this bike back to town and then return it to the young lady?"

The boy nodded. "Just tell me the address," he grinned at her. "I'll be there, I'll be there for sure."

Katarina murmured the number and the street and realized only then that it could mean nothing but more trouble; while the older one reminded her of her father, the younger one did not remind her of her brother, but of a fellow student who locked her in a dark classroom at the school dance and insisted on kissing her. He let her out only when she started screaming. Once she had dried her tears, straightened her clothes, smoothed her hair as best she could, and returned to the ballroom, the boys' mutterings behind her back were so unpleasant that she soon left and went home.

The young policeman nodded contentedly, and on catching her worried look he grinned: "Don't worry! I'll remember. I remember everything. Don't worry, hah, hah . . ."

Thus, of course, she worried even more, but she thought that perhaps that was precisely what the boy wanted, and that therefore she should not show how worried she really was.

Her way of thinking was perhaps correct, but it did not make her situation any easier. And while sitting in the squad car, which was driving fast back to town, Katarina thought to herself that it was her unease that had made her overlook how the policeman had put his arm around her shoulders and taken her to the car without her really wanting that.

"What do you do in life, baby?" asked the policeman without taking his eyes off the road.

"I make music," she said. "For ballets."

"For dancing?"

Katarina considered his words. For dancing . . . none of the answers were correct. Of course, music for ballets is music for dancing. But he probably means dance music. And her music would not seem to him that kind, she thought.

"It should be heard first," she said cautiously.

"Sure! Sure!" He became enthusiastic. "I'd love to!"

Katarina wondered whether it had really sounded like an invitation or whether the man had only made clever use of the opportunity. She did not want it to sound like an invitation. But now it would be difficult to back off, it seemed to her.

And so they went to her studio, to the little rented room where she spent all her days and nights, and which smelled of canned food and welding. She pressed buttons and let sounds out of speakers. He sat on an upturned beer crate, raising his eyebrows to the rhythm of the music.

"Do you like it?" she asked eventually, when she could no longer bear the grotesqueness of the situation.

He shook his head. She knew; her father would not have liked it either. Actually, she did not like it herself. The sounds were all wrong. It was not easy to find the right ones. Although she searched a lot. After all, that was the reason why she had stopped by the people gathering around the corpse. The murmur, she thought. And turned off the switches.

"Never mind," added the policeman immediately, in a conciliatory tone. "People also enjoy things they don't like. Death, for instance, nobody likes death. But all the same, quite a lot of people gather around a dead body. They've got their reasons." He looked at her carefully. "You had yours, too."

Katarina could do nothing but nod.

"Do you like looking at dead bodies?" he asked. "I can take you to the morgue if you want. I've got friends there. They let me in whenever I want. You know, a job's a job. The best of them's bad, and mine's not the best."

With alarm Katarina realized that neither the thought of corpses carefully laid out nor the man's worn-out chatter were as repulsive as they should have been.

"I'd rather not, thank you," she said politely.

He nodded.

"I didn't think you would," he said. "I imagined you that way. You would and you wouldn't. Both at the same time. Yes, that's right. Yes, I like that. Tell me," he changed the tune, "why did you turn off the music?"

"I don't want to be keeping you," tried Katarina.

"Aw, come on, who said anything about keeping me? I like being here. You aren't telling me to go, are you?"

grinned the policeman. When in response Katarina maintained a numb silence, he said cajolingly: "Aren't we going to dance?"

"I don't dance."

"Yes, I know that. Even if you did, you wouldn't. Right?"

"I just wouldn't," said Katarina. "There is no if."

"U-huh," said the policeman and started to unbuckle his belt. "So, are you going to tell me about your father? Have you got something to drink?"

"What are you doing?" asked Katarina.

"Doing? Nothing," the policeman was surprised and pulled the shirt out of his trousers. "Do you want me to keep my boots on? Or will I remind you of him more without them? What do you think?"

"I think it's time for you to leave," said Katarina. She went to the door and opened it.

"Oh, come on," he laughed. "I'm in no hurry, like I said before. The party hasn't even started yet, why should I go anywhere. Come on, girl, relax. If you don't feel like it any longer, we can go see dead bodies, like I told you before. Just tell me what you want. Everything's possible. I can arrange a lot of things. You won't be the first. Just tell me. You can't just sit there waiting for me to guess what it is you want."

"I want you to go," said Katarina weakly.

The policeman looked at her in surprise.

"I don't understand," he said.

"I want you to go," she repeated.

"Well, if that's what you want, I'll go," the policeman shrugged his shoulders. He went to the door without tucking his shirt back in, carrying his belt in his hand. "I'm going, I'm going. I didn't realize," he looked at Katarina, "we didn't understand each other."

Katarina felt that she could still come out on top and she could not contain herself.

"Didn't we?" she asked.

"Mhm," said the policeman, already paying more attention. "I see. Of course, I'm old. These are new things. You like to be left alone, don't you?"

"That's how I live," said Katarina. "Alone."

"Is it difficult?" asked the policeman.

"You get used to it," said Katarina. "You're not alone, are you?" she added.

"Me? No, not at all!" the policeman warmed to the subject. "I've got a wife. And two daughters. Great girls. Blondes. Want to see their pictures?" He was already taking the wallet from his pocket.

"No, no." Katarina felt the beginning of nausea. "No, please don't."

"No? OK then. Another time," the policeman said, surprised.

There won't be any other time, thought Katarina as she was walking downstairs at the policeman's side. Because, if nothing else, every other time has to have a first time. And here there had been no first time. Only an offered ride home that she had not refused.

At the door, the policeman turned to face her. "By the way," he said, "where's your father now?"

"He's gone," said Katarina.

"Gone away? Ugh," the policeman made a face. "You'll find another man, don't worry. There's plenty of them in the world!"

"To tell you the truth," said Katarina, "I'm not really interested in that." And she pondered to what extent her statement was a lie. Not very much, she thought, and added to herself that she might feel better if it had not been a lie at all. Take, for instance, this policeman. An interesting man, perhaps, if you are capable of noticing.

"What are you interested in, then? Girls?" said the policeman, less affectedly than she expected.

Katarina shook her head.

"Oh, come on," said the policeman. "It can't be that you don't like this."

With one hand he turned her around, pushing her against the wall, and with his other hand he reached between her legs.

Katarina closed her eyes, then opened them again. Nothing. The hand was in the same place as before. She had not dreamed it. And she did not feel anything. Only the moisture oozing down the wall and seeping through her T-shirt. She looked up the stairs and saw the wet traces on the window. The rain. She wondered whether she had put her bicycle in a dry place. And remembered where she had left it.

"Let go of me," she said, and then again, louder, "let go!"

"You don't like it?" said the policeman, taken aback.

She shook her head.

"Aw, come on," said the policeman, "I know every woman likes it."

And he reached between her legs again.

"Not like this," said Katarina and pushed him away. "I can do it better myself."

"Show me."

"Are you crazy?"

"A little. The doctors said I'm not dangerous. I got back into uniform. Only they won't give me a gun. Public opinion, they say. You have to be very careful. The press is poisonous. Nobody likes policemen. Come on, show me how you do it."

"But you've got a gun," said Katarina.

"This? It's a water gun. A toy. It doesn't even squirt well. Come on, show me."

He is crazy, thought Katarina. And God knows if the pistol is really just a water gun. My father used to say that everything was just a game, too. And then it was not. It was for real. Too real.

The hall door slowly, squeakingly opened. These gothic sounds would have been funny if they had not always been the same. The younger policeman came panting in, dragging Katarina's bicycle along.

"The rain," he explained cheerfully, "it's raining. I barely escaped it." But he had not escaped entirely. His trouser legs were dripping. With interest his eyes traveled up and down Katarina's body, tense, against the wall, and he did not seem to notice the hand caught between her legs.

"Hey, listen," protested the older one, "you can't do that. We agreed . . ."

"We agreed," the younger one interrupted, "that we both had two hours, and if one didn't make it, the other one could give it a try."

"That's just it," objected the older one, "two hours . . ."

"How long do you think it takes to get here by bike from that damn village? More than two hours, I tell you. Look at the watch! I went as fast as I could, but I couldn't make it here on time. It's two hours twenty-five minutes, see for yourself."

"That's because of the music," the older one bowed his head, "she played me some sort of music." And he withdrew his hand.

"Well, what's better than music?" grinned the younger one and with outstretched arms offered the bicycle to Katarina. "Do you want it or not?"

"What?" said Katarina.

"Well, this," smiled the policeman, "the bike." And he burst into laughter as if he had told a good joke.

"It's mine, isn't it?" asked Katarina, took it by the crossbar, and leaned it against the wall.

"Do you always leave it like that? You don't lock it?"

"Yes," said Katarina. "Nothing's ever happened."

"But it will, it will," nodded the younger one with an air of an expert. "Baby, you need a cop. Otherwise you'll find yourself with nothing to put between your legs."

"Sorry, but what you're saying is vulgar," said the older one. "You're disgracing the uniform."

"The uniform? I'd take it off, it's wet, but it's cold in here. No offense meant. What about you? Did you behave? Was everything OK?" He turned to Katarina and she, without thinking, nodded.

"More or less," she said and paused, as if there were too much to add if she really got started. "Relatively."

"I thought so," the younger one said ambiguously. "Anyway, he's going now, aren't you? You're going, right?"

"Going?" the older one appeared confused. "Going where? Not out in this rain?"

"I was out there, and I survived," said the younger one pathetically, as if he really meant it. "Yes, survived and came here. And here I am."

"You've got nothing going here," said the older one. "She needs a father, not a brother."

"And you're a father."

"I'm like a father."

True, thought Katarina, how true. Like Father. The same. He thinks he understands. He thinks he knows. But he doesn't know. He doesn't understand.

She heard the drumming of the rain against the courtyard window and the echo of the drops falling into the puddle below the staircase. Good sounds, familiar sounds. That did not have to be searched for in electronics. That were always there. In every rainstorm. And she thought how soothing it was that nothing changed. Now they were talking about her, and just a short while ago somebody was pushing his hand between her legs, but everything remained the same. And when she goes up to her room, it will also be the same. The same smells. The same music on her tapes. Everything so reliably the same.

"Wait, wait a moment," she heard the younger one say, "don't start with that crap. Now it's time for fair play, right? You go, I stay."

"Ask her," she heard the older one say. "Isn't it fair to ask her?"

"Then I will," she heard the younger one say. "Well, what do you say? Should he go, or does he have anything left to do here?"

What's the difference, thought Katarina. If the older one goes, the younger one stays, and vice versa, but what's the difference? They're both strangers, neither of them is her father or her brother.

As if it would be any different, she then said to herself, if one of them really were her father or brother. Everything would still be in the same place, even that hand between her legs. It is all the same if they stay or go, so let them go, so that I will not have to know how much it really is the same, even if it is different. Complicated, beyond doubt.

"Thank you both for bringing me here," she said.

"Oh, that's all right!" said the younger one quickly, as if he had all that much to do with it. "Besides, let me tell you, baby, this isn't the last stop yet."

"Nothing doing with her, I tell you," the older one tried to calm him down. "I've tried everything. The broad's a special sort. I can't quite make out what she actually wants."

If this was everything, thought Katarina, then I want exactly what I already have: nothing.

"That's you, and I'm me," said the younger one. "Besides, you're always forgetting something: I'm younger. Younger. You know, the fast life. So?" he turned to Katarina again.

"Yeah, right, live fast, die young, and be a goodlooking corpse. But they also say experience comes with age," added the older one in an erudite manner.

I've heard that before, thought Katarina.

"And you never stop making use of it," rebuked the younger one.

"Sure I do," protested the older one. "You don't know how long it's been since I did it last!"

"I do know," said the younger one. "Your last one hasn't even dried yet. You know what the guys that put her in the hearse said? That it was a real relief loading one that wasn't bloody, for a change."

The face covered with wet heather appeared in front of Katarina's eyes. She waited for a denial that would indicate to what extent she had misunderstood them, but the older policeman just thoughtfully shifted his gaze from his young partner to her and back. His eyes traveled back and forth, as if following a tennis ball flying over a net, and Katarina felt dizzy; she could feel the weakness arising from her spine, her fingertips grazed the banister, and she found herself staring at the chipped terrazzo on the floor.

"What's the matter?" she heard above her. "Anything wrong? They all get what they want. Just tell me what you want and you'll get it. We're real white knights, aren't we?"

Katarina felt the metal edge of the banister cutting into her forehead, but the feeling did not have the quality of pain, just discomfort. She caught the liquid trickling down her face on her tongue. A familiar taste.

"What if we called it a day," she heard the younger one. "This is getting too wild for me. So you won't stick it in. I didn't either."

The older one muttered something unintelligible.

Katarina turned to face them, but she could not open her eyes fully, they were glued together.

"I can't see," she said. She could feel a soft tissue settling on the cut, some sort of cloth, increasingly heavy.

"The blood should be washed away," she heard the older one say.

"We'd need some water," she heard the younger one say.

"There's plenty of water," she heard the older one say, "today there's water everywhere."

"Let's do this and get going," she heard the younger one say. "I don't feel like anything no more. I don't like blood. Now water, that's OK, I can deal with that."

Katarina ran the back of her hand across her eyes and saw the older one aiming his gun at her. At her eyes.

No, she thought, oh no.

The squirt hit her face. At first it seemed as if something were completely wrong: it should be flowing in the other direction, she thought. Then she realized that it was really a water gun. Pink streaks stained her skirt.

The younger one began to laugh.

"What?" she said.

"Nothing," he said. "it's just funny. Now I feel a bit more relaxed. Before, I was almost sick. I like water better than blood."

Katarina reached to her forehead and touched what had been laid on it. It felt so rough to the touch that she wished it were already part of her body. But perhaps it would not have been any different even then.

"You can keep the handkerchief," said the older one. "Imagine what my wife would say if I brought it home all bloody."

"Let the women talk," said the younger one. "What do they know."

"Some macho talk, huh?" the older one smirked in Katarina's direction. "Impressed?"

"Tired," she said. And it seemed to her that that was in reality about all she felt.

"Well, anyway," the older one shrugged his shoulders, "we'll be going now. Keep the handkerchief. It might come in handy. Chew on it a bit, up in your room, when you're alone. To get the taste of blood on your taste buds."

"I know what blood tastes like," she said after the men going through the door.

The older one, who was walking behind, turned and nodded. Now his face looked tired, ashen, and Katarina remembered her father's face, covered with a plastic sheet. Now that she knew she was going to be left alone, the similarity was no longer so insufferable.

"Yours," he said. "Yours. But have you ever licked someone else's?"

Katarina shook her head. What was this man saying?

"Go back to your machines, girl," said the policeman. "And don't think that any two ever taste the same. No. Not any. Good luck with your music."

Katarina watched them turning around a corner. Now, from the back, she could not distinguish with certainty which one was the younger and which one the older. It was getting dark, they were of the same height, and their uniforms were identical.

It had stopped raining. In the puddles on the sidewalk the reflections of the streetlamps being turned on were faintly glimmering.

No, thought Katarina, no.

She ran after the policemen.

The younger one was already sitting in the car, while the older one was unlocking the door on the driver's side. "Hi there, girl!" he cried cheerfully. "Want to go for another ride?"

Katarina pretended she had not heard him.

"Can I ask you something?" she asked.

"You're already asking," replied the policeman. "Go ahead."

"What really happened to that woman?"

"Which woman?" the policeman knitted his eyebrows.

"The drowned woman."

"Oh, that one!" a smile spread across his face. "I see.

Nothing terrible. She just drowned. I'll send you the death certificate, if you're really interested."

And he offered her his hand. Katarina looked at it. A hand like any other, she thought. Why shouldn't I shake it? Really, I could.

But she could not.

"You were just joking before, weren't you?"

"About what?" the policeman did not understand. He was still offering his right hand. Katarina remembered how this hand was caught between her legs. The feeling seemed far away and utterly unrecognizable. One of the many. Like the metallic taste of an empty spoon in her mouth.

"Well, about the last time you did it. He was teasing you, wasn't he?"

The policeman watched her and slowly let his hand drop by his side.

"Good girl," he said. "Sure, he was teasing me. I haven't done it for ages. Here, this is my phone number. I have to go now, can't keep the boy waiting. If he gets jealous, he'll turn me in, he can make up one hell of a story, about things I do, nasty stuff. But call me some time. My wife's got cooking class on Tuesdays and Thursdays. I can come to your place. If you want, I'll let you bite me, till you draw blood. You should really try that once."

He smiled at her and laid his hand on her shoulder. Now he really looked like a father—not her father. A father like fathers in general. Those one can see in the park, lovingly explaining the facts of life to their children. And she did not know why he suddenly seemed so familiar. Perhaps because he was leaving.

Maybe that's it, thought Katarina. The taste of blood, someone else's. Maybe that is the thing that cannot be expressed by sounds, the thing that is missing.

She took the proffered slip of paper and nodded.

"Perhaps I will," she said. And thought: My life will change. I can feel it will.

The policeman also nodded.

"Sure you will," he said. "I knew you'd see me again. Everybody ends up liking me. In the beginning there's some harsh words, quarrels, there's sometimes even blood, I'm not saying there isn't, but in the end everybody likes me."

He got in and started the car. He turned toward Katarina and pressed his lips against the glass. Between his lips, his breath left an oval mark. Then he drove off fast, so that mud splashed from under the wheels.

On her way back Katarina could feel the rainwater penetrating the soles of her shoes. So what, she thought. It's only water. Nothing dangerous. It dries and then it's all right. It doesn't leave stains.

When she entered the hallway, she realized somebody had stolen her bicycle. On the place by the wall where she had left it, nothing remained but a puddle.

■ □ ■ □ ■

SCRATCHES ON THE BACK

I WAS GAZING AT THE STAINS THE RED WINE HAD LEFT ON the rug. I had purchased it in San Sebastian, a mountain town in southern Mexico. The man sold it for a few dollars and a few pesos after a half-hour haggle, and then chased after me explaining that he had calculated everything again and that I still owed him twenty cents. Twenty cents! And this after dropping the price by more than half, to thirty dollars, thanks to that long, and for me, painful bargaining session. All right, I thought, and gave him a quarter, now try to exchange this change at a bank here. The man flipped the coin and chuckled. As I watched him smile it occurred to me that there might have been some detail, worth more than twenty cents, that had escaped me. But since I could not figure out how he had conned me, I didn't feel too badly about it, especially since the rug was really cheap and beautiful, too. Well, it was, till last night.

I tried to imagine the stains were Rorschach blots, and studied them closely to find out something about myself. All I could figure out was that I had invited the wrong people to the party last night. People who didn't appreciate hand-woven rugs made of the mountain-goat hair. People who let wine splash over the rims of their glasses while they went on about their adventures and waving their hands in the air.

Some adventures. People obviously think that they can turn every nothing into something if they pump it up enough. And this usually requires a lot of gesticulation. The results were staring at me from the rug.

I had only myself to blame. I could have chosen not to throw a party. I used up my whole supply of wine, sacrificed the cheese a friend had brought from his skiing holiday in Switzerland, and discovered that my Spanish olives were being lobbed into an empty bowl. It was, I guess, a spontaneous game that had broken out among my guests. And to top off the evening, the girl I had thrown the party for left before it was over. And not alone either.

It occurred to me that now was the time to play one of the most precious records in my collection. A record I had not heard in a long time. Which one, though? I went through the list. It's fairly difficult to make a choice when you have as many records as I do. I'll have two thousand soon. Lately my friends have been desperate to sell me the records I used to beg for, and for which I had sometimes offered enormous sums. My friends were panicking over the end of an era, and the thought that very soon records would mean nothing at all. That their fate would be that of the 8mm films and the Beta videocassettes. These friends have all acquired CD players and are now in the process of building their libraries from scratch. They buy all the CDs they can get their hands on. And they keep telling me that I'm behind the times. All right, let it be. Behind the times, but I can listen to the rarities whenever I feel like it.

Finally I selected a bootleg edition of the Smiths, a double live album entitled *Never Had No One Ever*. Slightly pathetic, I admit, but suitable for an evening like this.

I sat down in an easy chair, piled foreign magazines

next to it, cut myself some more cheese and poured myself a glass of wine from one of the many uncorked, and still relatively full, bottles. The wine isn't as tasty, but drinking it is easier that pouring decent wine down the drain. Then I dropped the needle onto the record.

The audience had not yet finished applauding when the doorbell rang.

No, I thought, not now. I had spent the whole afternoon cleaning up the mess and not one volunteer had appeared, though several had promised to help. And now, when everything was clean (except for the Mexican rug), somebody decided to show up.

I turned down the volume and called out: "Who is it?"

"It's me," said a female voice from the other side of the door.

Who me? I didn't recognize the voice. But I felt too dumb yelling back: who's that . . . me? So I groaned quietly, killed the record, and opened the door.

It was Diana, Peter's wife. Diana and Peter and I had gone to university together. They weren't exactly my kind of people, too complex for my practical mind, I'd say, but we knew each other, and for a while after graduation Peter and I worked for the same architectural firm, and everybody predicted he'd be a success because he was a talented architect, although he did think in a somewhat unusual manner. Or maybe that was precisely the reason. Then Peter's career was ruined: his grandfather died and left him a shack in some godforsaken place. He took us there for a picnic, the whole office, but the atmosphere wasn't exactly the best, since everybody kept glancing at their mud-splashed cars and wondering what scratches were hidden beneath the layers of mud. Even the most generous-minded were unable to call the track that led to his new property a road.

The building didn't charm the party either. Okay, it

was a romantic old ruin, I have to admit, suitable for fashion layouts, but it lacked practically all the necessities, and what features it did have would, in any event, have to be torn down and rebuilt.

Although the twenty or so architects gathered there shared this opinion with Peter, he didn't take us seriously. I can understand him in a way—on principle I don't believe a word my colleagues say—but this went way beyond understandable professional mistrust. The stones were practically falling out of their places, and water and electricity were far away. In short, the end of the world.

None of this seemed to bother Peter. He decided to move there (which we thought insane), leave his job (which we thought equally insane, but then again how could he travel to work . . . by tractor?), and renovate the house (which we thought, although necessary, totally impossible, since there was nothing to renovate; everything would have to be built anew. Besides, even if he decided to rebuild the place, how could he do it when the closest water main was some ten miles away?).

What was even more unusual was that Diana, his girlfriend through university, and some said since high school, and now an unemployed architect, was willing to go there with him. We found it understandable enough that Peter had gone out of his mind; after all, similar suicidal plans occurred every now and then to us too, when we were bent over the drawing desks in the office. Someone from the office once even applied for a UNESCO job that had to do with a water co-op project in the Solomon Islands, only to return after six months barely alive, ravaged by various tropical diseases. But then payday comes and you forget the worst, at least for a while.

But that Peter had managed to enthuse Diana about his crazy idea we could only explain by the fact that they, and she especially, had always been fervent in their belief in the so-called natural way of life: health foods, Oriental music, weird books, and reeking incense in their little room. (Some people thought that their somewhat anachronistic habits explained why they had fewer visitors than ordinary couples of their age, but Peter defended himself by explaining that they wanted to have a cozy atmosphere and that guests who were not able to appreciate this were not welcome anyway. I didn't worry about it; after all, I saw more than enough of Peter at work.)

I had seen Peter last about two years ago, when he came to the office to pick up his things, and discovered his desk was already occupied by an architecture graduate with enormous tits, who never wore a bra and was also in other ways very cosmopolitan, so that she turned everybody's head, except our boss, who we privately thought was gay anyway. Although he did talk about women a lot. Or maybe because he did—to trick us. So, Peter came to collect the few things that belonged to him, and I made one last attempt to convince him that he was making a big mistake, and should drop to his knees and beg the boss to take him back, and forget about the shack.

I should have known better. Peter looked at me condescendingly, and said: "Take a look at yourself, kid. You're being eaten up by the city. You're always gulping some sort of pills. This won't end well. If you're smart, you'll come with me. And that's exactly my advice to you: get away. It'll make everything so much easier."

I thought he was joking.

"But Peter, what am I supposed to do there? I'm a city person, and even if I wasn't . . . there's nothing there. Nothing."

"That's just the point. You can create everything. Everything's waiting for you. You'll be the center of the world."

I realized he wasn't joking; it was worse than I had thought. The man had obviously gone too deep into the Oriental literature I had occasionally noticed on his desk—and from which I quickly averted my eyes. In his inheritance he must have seen a kind of holy omen: the time had come, that's why he was in such a rush.

"Peter, don't do anything foolish," I said.

Peter grinned.

"We'll see who's being foolish," he said. "We'll see."

And he left.

I had not heard about him since, and, to be honest, I quickly forgot about him. Every now and then somebody at the office would mention Peter, as in: if the old man (meaning our boss) doesn't stop shoving his vision of the project down my throat, I'll just pack my things and take off like Peter. Peter became a mythical figure of sorts for his ex-colleagues, a man who had accomplished the incredible and superhuman, at least considering the circumstances in our office. The boss paid us well, and if somebody disagreed with his visions and told him so (or let it be understood through sketches), he packed their things for them. Nobody in our office ever resigned, we were dismissed, fired. Peter was the exception.

And now, here was Diana, whom I didn't know as a person, but only in relation to Peter, as his girlfriend and wife, even though we met almost a decade ago. She held beaten and bulging suitcases in both hands. I could ask only one question.

"What brings you here?" I asked her.

"I ran away from Peter," she said.

Ran away? Well, considering the circumstances that was no big wonder. Actually it was unusual that it had taken her so long. But why show up at my place?

I kept these thoughts to myself.

"Ran away?"

"He's gone nuts."

You're a little late with that discovery, babe, I thought.

"Crazy?" I was politely ignorant.

"Crazy. He's preoccupied with stuff. He can't get it out of his mind. It's impossible to do anything with him. Anything."

I had the feeling that this was her way of concealing something substantial, something that she had meant to say but then decided shouldn't be voiced.

"What's impossible?"

"I told you. Everything."

I considered probing further.

"Tell me," she then said, "have you ever been in a desert?"

"Yeah," I said. "Several times. First in Egypt. Then one winter in California. I have some wonderful slides. You might be interested in . . ."

She wasn't listening.

"With him it was like being in a desert," she said.

Of course, I thought. He obviously hadn't built a highway to his property. And they probably didn't have a tractor.

"Dull, huh?" I said.

She looked at me a bit puzzled.

"No, no. Just tiny little grains making up the whole. Like that."

Oh, I thought, it's a metaphor. I decided not to get involved in the conversation. I wasn't up to it.

"And what are you going to do now?" I asked.

"I'm going to stay with you for a while," she said.

"With me? Why me?"

"You were the only person who understood me."

Well, I couldn't handle it. No way.

"Me?"

"You. I remember how once we got drunk after class and went to the Tivoli park. We climbed the hill, away from everybody else, and I told you about my life. And you kept saying: yeah, I understand."

I couldn't say that it had never happened. But I didn't remember a thing. When I get so plastered that I end up in the woods with somebody else's woman, I understandably like to forget all about it as soon as I can.

"And that's why you came here," I said with understanding and incredulity.

"Because of that," she confirmed. "You have an apartment. And I heard that you don't have a woman who might have minded my arrival. A woman who might not understand. Or do you?" she looked at me intently.

"I don't," I admitted. Who the hell told her about my personal life? "Not now." Yes, this definitely sounded better.

"Then it's OK," she said. "Where can I sleep?"

I looked around my apartment. I saw what I already knew: I had only one bed.

"There," I said.

"Thanks," she said. "I knew you wouldn't turn me out onto the street. I won't stay long, just until I get my bearings."

"You can stay as long as you like," I said dully.

"Thank you," she said seriously. She never noticed the irony.

It is difficult to be sweet and kind after forsaking one's bed and spending the night in a hammock (another souvenir from Mexico, to which I had so far attributed aesthetic rather than practical value). Nevertheless, I made coffee for Diana, let her help herself to what was in the fridge, asked her about her plans (she didn't have any), and told her to take the spare keys if she went out, and then I rushed off to the office. On the way I kept wondering: what am I doing? have I gone crazy? I have never given the spare keys to any woman, if for no other reason than superstition, symbolism, and that sort of thing. Now this.

When I came home from work, Diana was gone. On

the kitchen table I found evidence that she had made lunch to the best of her abilities out of my supplies. I washed the dishes and started soaking the pan in which something unknown to me had burned. Then I fell into my easy chair and closed my eyes.

Diana came back toward evening, and when she woke me up she seemed in a good mood. She asked me how I felt and I told her that I was hungry. She disregarded the hint, or else genuinely failed to understand it. Surprised, she mentioned my fridge. When I opened it I wasn't surprised: it really was empty, as I had expected.

I told her the fridge was empty. She said it was obvious I had to go shopping. I knew that myself. I asked her where she had been all day. I was hoping she would say she had been visiting old friends, asking them if she could move in. She said she had been watching the traffic on Tito Street (or whatever it is called now). I could relate. When I came back from the California desert, I was perfectly capable of watching water flow for hours.

So I went to the store and bought a few essentials. At the cash register I met a woman I knew from the old days, and with whom I had halfheartedly been trying to get together—"but this time really"—for ages. She wasn't married either, and now worked in an office staffed by women. I was standing there with a basketful of pairs: two fruit yogurts, two cartons of juice, two avocados (when she saw the avocados, the cashier looked at me and I realized, against my will, that I must have paid her daily earnings for them). I remembered that Diana ate almost nothing but fruit in her university days, although the thing that had burned in my pan was certainly not fruit. At first I hoped my acquaintance wouldn't notice the couples in my basket. Then I reproached myself for being paranoid.

She didn't notice. However, she did ask me whether

we could get together some time. Sure, I murmured and decided that if she chose to tell me she was free tonight, I might respond by asking her whether she still lived with her mother in their one-room apartment. Luckily, she sensed my somewhat sour mood and dropped the subject. She told me to watch my health if I had become a vegetarian, and said good-bye with dignity. The two of us will never get together, never, I thought. We beat about the bush too much, we procrastinate too much. Real women simply knock on your door, and there they are in your bed. I felt like laughing out loud, and for a moment I thought of stopping in the bar next to the store to pull myself together a bit. Then I changed my mind. Diana will be waiting, I told myself, and went home. I had obviously gone bananas. But I consoled myself with the thought that I may have always been this way and had noticed it only recently.

And that was how it went. I'd go to work while Diana slept. When I got home she was nowhere to be seen. I would wash the dishes, do the shopping, listen to my records, or leaf through my books. Toward evening she'd return, take over the bathroom, and leave me squirming in front of the door, wondering whether I should go, toothbrush in my pocket, to the washroom in the bar on the ground floor of our building. After the end of the occupation, she'd go straight to bed. It seemed as if she slept some sixteen hours a day, and I would have believed that if I had not caught her standing by the window and staring out on the street almost every time I woke up in the middle of the night.

The first time I saw her, I asked her what she was doing, and she said nothing. (It also looked that way.) Then I thought that she could be waiting for someone. She sure is patient, waiting for him night after night. And then I decided I shouldn't leave myself out when speaking about patience. I was paying for all the food. Also the telephone bill was pretty large, considering I had broken all social contacts. And then there were the scratches that had started to appear on my records. I had a vague idea she might be listening to them while I was out, although I always found them in their proper alphabetical order. The scratches weren't the ones left when a needle is jolted; it looked as though a wild cat had slid across the record.

To find out what was going on I asked Diana to put on a record. When I saw the way she did it, a cold shiver ran up my spine. As she took the record out of its jacket, she ran her nails along its surface, so that they made a grating noise. I said nothing. The scratching spoke for itself. When I recovered, more or less, I asked her never to touch my records again. Never. She nodded in amazement and watched me as one might a moron, as if she were saying: but just a few moments ago you told me to put on the record.

I had not been able to avoid certain experiences with women, but I had long ago decided that I would never find myself living with one. How had this happened? Perhaps this was an irony of fate. So, I said to myself, this is what real life is like. Absentmindedly, I started to chuckle. Diana was watching me with growing horror. Well, let it be, I said to myself, let it be.

Two weeks later, after downing a bottle and a half of wine, and realizing that things had already started to become soothingly unimportant, Diana finally felt something and asked me what was wrong. Nothing, I told her, rather coldly. At first she nodded, as though satisfied, then she began to have doubts. She asked me to tell her what was wrong. But she phrased it in an unusual manner. She said:

"Since we're living together under the same roof I really don't see why you should try to conceal it from me when something goes wrong."

I don't know why I didn't hold back:

"Diana, it can't go on like this. You left Peter. OK, I would've done the same. You came to town. That's also OK, normal people live in cities. You came to stay the night. That's passable, we once knew each other and I live alone, there's enough room. Now you're here and you eat my food. OK, I have a heart of gold. In a way I feel fine being able to say to myself: you really are something, helping her out like this. But, Diana, something's not OK. This can't go on."

"What can't go on?" she asked, surprised.

"Well, it isn't natural. We're living together and what? You're not my sister. You're not my daughter. You're not my mother. You're not my wife. What will people think? It isn't quite normal that a woman is living with me just like that. For one night, OK . . ." Here I bit my tongue.

"Have you got another woman?" asked Diana.

"What do you mean—another? Who's the first?"

"Well, me," she said, slightly offended.

"But—Diana! You've been here for two weeks and we haven't even touched each other! You're not my woman, even if it looks that way from the outside. Have you forgotten?"

"What are we then?" she asked simply.

I shrugged my shoulders. Friends? Strange friends to be living together and yet not really exchange a word for a week. Are we sharing the household and nothing else? But what's being shared? I provide the food, do the cooking and the cleaning, and she eats. So?

"I don't know," I admitted. "But I can only see as my woman the woman who . . ."

"Who?" Diana urged me to go on.

"Well, who I sleep with."

"Oh," said Diana, "I knew we'd come to that."

Acquiring the reputation of a sexual harasser will be a small price to pay to get rid of her, I thought. Now she'll call me a pig and pack her bags.

"I knew it even back then, when we hid in the woods in the park," she added.

A wild reputation since the early age, I thought with complacent irony. No wonder she couldn't bear to live under the same roof with me.

"Well, then," decided Diana calmly, "I'll sleep with you."

And before I managed to respond she slipped her dress over her head. There was no self-consciousness in her gesture. She was like a child who doesn't know what she's doing, but clearly understands what she has to do. The skin that suddenly glistened before my eyes drained all the power I might have mustered to defend myself. I wanted to say: no, no, no. I wanted to ask: what are you doing? But I wasn't fast enough, and then it was too late.

When, after two weeks of sleeping in a hammock, one feels a solid bed underneath one's body, life looks brighter in the morning, no matter what had happened during the night. To tell the truth, I didn't know exactly what had happened. The only thing I knew for certain was that in the morning Diana got up first, made breakfast, brought it to me in bed, did the dishes, walked me to the door as I left for work, and kissed me good-bye on the cheek. I accepted all this with the resignation of a man facing a firing squad and wondering only whether it would take long.

Perhaps it was just a dream, I thought as I stood in front of the bathroom mirror washing away the blood that had caked on my face over night. The scratches were just on the surface, but they were long and equally distributed along both cheek. After I had washed my face and lathered on some coldcream, the scratches were bare-ly visible. And the ones on my back were difficult to notice, I reassured myself. A dream, yes, a dream, that's the right word.

When I came home, with a bundle of blueprints under my arm, because I had not been able to do much except stare at nothing and wonder what I had gotten myself into, the table was laid, and lunch was cooked, full of ingredients I certainly did not have at home. I felt that the previous night had changed things drastically, but I didn't know why, let alone whether I really wanted that.

After lunch, over coffee (it was terrific, and I found it hard to believe that Diana used to be such a militant sup-porter of health foods, since she was capable of making such terrific coffee), Diana asked me to take her to the movies, claiming that she hadn't been to the cinema in years. Of course I told her yes, and asked her what she wanted to see. She said it didn't matter. All she wanted was to sit in a dark place and watch pictures flit across a screen.

I scanned the newspaper. I didn't recognize any of the films on the program, and the Kinoteka repertory theater was featuring a Bergman, and, considering the circum-stances, I found it completely inappropriate to take her to see that sort of film. So I chose the theater in my neigh-borhood, just a couple of minutes away, and which was showing a melodrama, which is, as far as I know, the genre that is close to everyone.

The idea was not as good as I had thought. Diana obvi-ously enjoyed herself, much more than I did. The first mistake I made was to forget that I would probably run into the same people I always see there. That's what hap-pens when you live in the same area for decades and fre-quent the same cinema. So I kept nodding in a friendly fashion in all directions, but quickly realized that they weren't so much interested in greeting me as they were in checking out my companion. Just as the situation was becoming unbearable, the film thankfully started and we were cloaked in darkness. The plot centered on what you could call a young middle-aged man and woman who have to share an apartment because of a shortage in housing. They aren't attracted to each other, and the predicament made me nervous, especially toward the middle of the film, when, apparently out of boredom, the couple decides to spend a night under the same blanket, to coin a phrase. The whole thing ended much worse than I had anticipated, because finally she (in a scene shot disgustingly slowly, so that it almost made me sick) cuts his throat while he's sleeping, takes all his money, and goes off God-knows-where.

After the film ended I kept glancing at Diana, but she gave no sign of having recognized herself in the film in any way. (And I didn't know whether to relax or worry.) Two friends from elementary school, whom I had not seen in a long time, and whom I would have given the world not to have seen at that moment, tapped me on the shoulder. It turned out they had been sitting behind me the whole time wondering whether it was me in front of them. When they finally agreed that it was me, they— judging by their looks appraising Diana—started guessing whether she had come to the cinema with me or had accidentally purchased a ticket for the seat next to the good-for-nothing that I was in grade school. (And probably still am.)

Well, they talked to me about the impression the film had made on them, but they kept looking at Diana, who smiled in a puzzled way, as if she didn't understand why they were staring at her. (Maybe she really didn't?) For the sake of old friendship I stood it for a while, then told them to excuse me, since I had to go. They didn't object, but looked slightly surprised and disappointed when Diana followed me resignedly. Obviously they'd been hoping Diana was standing next to me because she had nothing better to do that evening. I have to admit it was difficult to hold back the feeling of triumph. We males take turns winning, and this time I was the victor, I thought with vanity, and at the same time I knew that my thoughts didn't have all that much to do with the real situation. But the feeling was pleasant anyway, until I heard one of them ask, after we had gone some distance:

"Is this his girlfriend?"

"He doesn't have a girlfriend," said the other one.

"I mean his ex."

"He doesn't have an ex either."

And they started to snicker.

The following days floated by. I existed without weight. I was sleeping in my hammock again. I didn't let Diana near me, although I have to admit that wasn't difficult, since she made no advances. If she was at home, I would put earphones on and listen to some blistering music. If she wasn't around, I would sit by the window and watch the street. There was nothing there, but that didn't bother me. I found it logical, natural. The work I brought home from the office, because I couldn't do any work there, lay in a corner. I didn't touch it, except in the morning when I took it back to work.

It didn't take long before my boss told me that it was obvious I wouldn't be asking for extra time off this year since I couldn't even handle the regular work, let alone finish something ahead of time. I kept a dignified silence and waited for him to finish, and then I started drawing blueprints, so hastily that I immediately caught my sleeve in some utensils and spilled ink over the only blueprint I had almost finished. While the black liquid dripped onto my shoes I considered whether I should quickly write my letter of resignation, or let my boss do it instead.

The boss watched from the doorstep, not saying anything. When I managed to pull myself together and look at him, he nodded seriously. Then he slowly turned around and left. I felt as though I had blushed from head to toe. Calm, I said to myself, stay calm. It will pass.

Just like Diana's cooking and keeping house for me had passed. The very day after. I wondered why. It was either that she felt like my woman only the night I slept with her and she thought that she could do these things only as my woman, or else it was something else. The old atmosphere returned to the apartment, as if nothing had happened.

I wondered what to do. I felt that the price I had to pay for Diana's housekeeping services was too high. And besides that, I had managed on my own for quite a while. (Before Diana's arrival I had quite frequently thought that I had lived alone for too long. Now I realized I hadn't.) It couldn't last forever. The bathroom was occupied far too often. I wanted to listen to music over the loudspeakers, because I was sick and tired of earphones. Every now and then I wanted the option of bringing home some of my old girlfriends, who now looked strangely at me when we met in the street, while I greeted them mumbling something unintelligible instead of being witty and eloquent, as I used to be.

In short, with earphones on my ears I decided it was high time Diana went somewhere else. (Against my will I started believing that her going back to Peter would be a wonderful solution, if only because it would take her far from my apartment.) The only thing that marred my satisfaction at this conclusion was the sad fact that nothing of the sort would occur to her and that I would have to clarify the situation. And if I remembered the outcome of my last attempt at explaining to her the unnaturalness of our relationship, I lost the will to give it another try. Who knows how it would end this time, since things seem to repeat themselves like a bad joke. But, as the saying goes, there is a force that draws a man to look over the edge of the abyss.

So I slipped off the earphones and went searching for Diana. She was not in the living room, nor in the bedroom, nor in the kitchen (not that I found the latter surprising). I went to the bathroom and saw light seeping through from underneath the door.

I decided to wait for Diana to finish whatever she was doing, and went back to my armchair and started leafing through the magazines. But it soon seemed as if I had been waiting for an eternity. I went back to the bathroom door and leaned my ear against the wood.

Nothing; the water wasn't running, I couldn't hear Diana. She might have simply left the light on and gone out, as she was wont to do, I thought.

I knocked.

I heard nothing for the longest time. Then Diana said: "Yeees?"

I was embarrassed. I shouldn't have to ask permission to enter any room in my apartment, but on the other hand I couldn't just waltz in as though we were . . . well, intimate. So, what to do? Should I ask her what she was doing? If she's doing something a person normally does in a washroom, then she might think I'm a) stupid or b) vulgar. But I can't stand in front of this door forever. After all, it is my door.

At that moment Diana opened the door.

"Come in," she said.

When a person finds his own bathroom strange and unknown he's far gone, I thought. And that's how it was. The shelf, filled up till then by objects well known to me (my toothbrush, my toothpaste, my shaving foam, my razor, my Chaz aftershave, my comb, and a few other things) was now crowded with face powders, lipsticks, and makeup unknown to me.

The fact that these things were here now without my ever having seen them before was not the only thing that was unusual. I was also surprised that I had never seen any traces of them on Diana. I mean, she was never made up, or anything. She was, as far as I knew, a sort of health fiend, and cosmetics weren't supposed to be part of her life, at least not in such quantities. And that was the way I liked it: women seemed more natural to me without paints. Without makeup, women were the antithesis of the artificial, distorted towns we created at work— and I would go to the ends of the earth to find this essence.

"What's all this, Diana?" I asked, somewhat idiotically.

"Makeup," said Diana kindly and motioned that I should come closer and take a look at it.

Instead of bending over the shelf, as she might have expected, I stared at her. Yes, I was seeing right. She was made up. Her lips were wine red, her cheeks pale as linen, and her eyes shadowed by dark patches. I had seen a face like this just once before. But that was a man. An opera singer or something. Mephistopheles, I believe.

"You use these things?" I said, incredulously. "But I never saw you . . ."

"You couldn't have," she confirmed seriously. "It stays behind this door."

I don't know whether she splashed water onto her face to make me understand the meaning of her words or because it was simply the next step in some process. I understood that she put on makeup, then she washed it off and came out no different than before. Those long hours in the bathroom made a certain sense, although quite candidly, it wasn't evident to me.

"I see," I lied.

She looked at me and nodded. Obviously, she believed me. The world, she probably thought, is an orderly place. He understands me, I understand him, he understands himself, I understand myself. But I didn't understand her and she didn't understand me and I didn't understand myself and she didn't . . .

I stopped. Had I gone nuts?

"Diana," I started, "Diana . . ." And I felt I was getting stuck here. That I wasn't going to get anywhere. Again.

"Don't say anything," she interrupted me. "I know. I know why you're here."

She knows? I was terrified.

"I know," she said. "You're sad. Lonely. Unhappy. Troubled by your work. Work, work, work. All day long. You bring it home. You can't live this way."

That is the way most adults live, I thought, and it's just by chance you aren't one of them. Maybe it would have been better for you if you had been one of them. Maybe then we'd understand each other.

What nonsense. I knew: although all this was true, it still didn't prove that the way I lived was the way to live. That was what it was all about.

"You need comfort," she continued. "Too much work."

"What comfort?" I asked.

Diana looked at me with understanding.

"Comfort, thy name is woman," she said. It sounded like some cheap Italian movie.

"Is that so?" I asked with growing terror.

She nodded.

I knew what was going to follow. "No," I said, "no." But I guess I didn't sound convincing enough, since she smiled compassionately.

"I know you mean 'yes' even when you say 'no,'" she said. And moved closer.

No, I thought. No.

She didn't pull her dress over her head, since she wasn't wearing one. In all other ways it was like the first time. Yes, like the first time. I can't stop myself, I reproached myself with horror, while she drew her nails over my skin. No, I can't. And when her soaked makeup fell in drops on my shirt and then onto my skin, the feeling of humiliation and surrender in a strange and unfathomable way became increasingly familiar and bearable.

"Interesting," a voice said behind me, as I was bending over the drawing desk. "Interesting."

I turned around; of course, it was my boss. He was looking at my blueprint over my shoulder and nodding.

"I see you joined the avant-garde," he said gently. "Opus zero. Not bad. Perfect performance."

I shrugged. There was nothing to say.

"Who was it that said that every building grows out of the first architect's line on the paper?" asked the boss. "I wouldn't want our office to be responsible for the extinction of Slovenians. You know what people say, first you need a home, then you can have children."

I started feeling around for a pencil. I couldn't find one.

"Yes, inspiration," the boss nodded with solemnity. "Every masterpiece starts with divine inspiration."

"Boss, don't tease me," I sighed. "Do I deserve this?"

"I don't know," the boss said. "But I'm sure you don't deserve what I give you every first of the month."

"What do you mean?" I played innocent.

The boss smiled at me coquettishly.

"Apparently I'll have to find a replacement for you," he said in a friendly way. "Of course, that shouldn't be too difficult; young female graduates constantly knock on my door. Begging me for a job. Willing to do anything. Young, bosomy, not too overdressed. So, maybe they can't draw anything—we both know what blockheads taught them. But they can still be of some other use. At least that. What about you? What can I do with you?"

"Boss, it hurts me to hear you talk this way," I said slowly. I didn't think he was going to go for it. But at least I had to try.

"Of course, of course," he was all understanding. "It's hard when somebody takes your place because—how shall I put it—they can offer their boss the kind of services you can't. Well, we could still smooth things over if you tried a little harder . . ."

I was wondering whether he wanted to lure me into his bed and was just trying to veil his proposition with all his talk about women, or whether he was—which would be after all proper—advising me to actually draw something when I stepped behind my drawing board.

"I'm trying," I said.

The boss looked at me with interest.

"It's hard to imagine how much work you would do if you didn't try," he said.

"You don't value my work enough, boss," I said.

He didn't think it worthwhile to comment. I decided to go on the offensive. Considering the circumstances, I had nothing to lose.

"Go ahead and tell one of those girls fresh from university to come up with a serious project. Let's say a new town district, like South Cross. You know, functional and one with environment, as they say," I quickly added. And waited. If he has an answer to this, I'm done for at the office, I thought.

He didn't hesitate.

"There isn't a woman who could do that, even if she had three degrees," he said harshly. "All they know about towns is where the boutiques are."

I drew a breath of relief. Not only was I staying at the office, but the boss was obviously on our side, among the wholesome and energetic phallocrats. There could be no doubt about his sexual orientation. And so he'll probably understand if I start explaining to him that I have a new woman who's wearing me out so that I have no strength left for real work—but very soon I'm going to throw her out of the apartment and make up for lost time.

"Sometimes, however," he added, "someone who lives in the countryside understands cities. More than you do. Who would've thought it."

I didn't understand.

"What are you talking about?"

"What I mean," said the boss slowly, "is that I'm giving the South Cross project to Peter."

"Peter? Boss, Peter doesn't want anything to do with architecture anymore." I was stunned.

"Maybe he doesn't," the boss conceded. "But, if I'm to use a popular saying again, money doesn't stink. Everybody wants it. Every time I call Peter to suggest that he take on a project that you, my professionals, can't tackle, he agrees. And, behold the wonder, he does it better than you, who still consider yourselves architects. An upside-down world, isn't it?"

It is upside-down, but, considering my circumstances, I didn't pay much attention to this fact, or to Peter's sudden metamorphosis from a hermit into an active architect, although still in a godforsaken place (but with a telephone!). I had enough troubles of my own. If that's the way things are, I thought, I'm through at the office. And if that's how it is, I thought, I'll be out of work, and I'll need consolation. Comfort, thy name is . . .

Yes, I remembered that I had Diana at home and that lunch would be waiting for me, like this morning's breakfast, and Diana would want to wash out this wound just as she had wanted to wash out the scratches on my back, though she pretended not to know their origins.

And then I remembered that Diana was Peter's wife, and so everything came full circle. And at the same time it occurred to me that Peter's taking over my work also meant I would be able to talk to him. Tell him what was going on. (Or better yet, ask him what was going on.) Maybe he knew something that I didn't. And even if he doesn't: when things are said out loud they sometimes start to fall into place.

"Boss, I probably have a right to a last wish."

"A cigarette?" asked the boss.

For a second I was tempted to imply that I wished to take something else into my mouth in farewell. But I didn't summon up the courage. Your bourgeois upbringing shows, I reproached myself. You always watch your manners. Why didn't you get married, if that's the way you are, and now you could be taking the children for a stroll, instead of traipsing around strange countries?

"No. Peter's phone number," I said.

"Are you going to appeal to the good old days? To the former friendship?" the boss asked me.

"We were never really friends," I said. And maybe we never will be, I thought.

"What else then?" he asked. "How are you going to stop him?"

"I won't have to stop him. He won't want to come to town. You remember him."

"Well, I won't make him come to town," said the boss. "He does all the work at his place. He has a PC. And he sends his plans by a modem."

It sounded like science fiction.

"Boss, you're making it up," I said in disbelief. "You mean, Peter has a PC? And a modem? Even I hardly know what it means, and I live in the big city."

"Yeah, it's funny," said the boss. "When I talked him into taking the first assignment, I had to drive up to his place. It was a nightmare. But I had to go up. You were somewhere in some Asian mountains at the time, and we were pressed for time. I took everything with me: the desk, paper, all the equipment. He said he'd do it, because he desperately needed a computer. I looked around me—he didn't even have a TV set, and now a computer. What for? So that he could catalogue all God's names. Absolute communication with Him. He said he couldn't do it without a PC. For this computer he had electricity installed, it must have cost him a fortune . . . I don't understand. My mother used to go to church every day, but I could understand that." He stopped and looked at me. "Do you understand?"

"Boss, I don't understand anything," I admitted. "I don't understand Peter, and I don't understand you. I don't even understand myself anymore. But I don't bother about it much. If I did, it would kill me."

The boss looked me in the eye for a long time.

"You used to be all right," he said finally. "It's a pity it's over between us. I'll give you a decent compensation package."

And he started leafing through his address book.

While I was dialing Peter's number, I felt as if I was calling another world. Well, in a way I was. I wouldn't want that world for my own. The telephone rang, and then for a long time there was nothing.

I listened, and then finally, I heard a voice. Yes, it was Peter. "Hello," he said.

"Peter, this is Roman."

"Oh, it's you. How are you?"

"Peter, I'm in trouble. I've been fired, you're going to take over my work, but that can't be helped, you know what the boss is like. I'm calling about something else: your wife is here."

I expected silence and an embarrassing tension, but I was wrong.

"I know she's there. And I know you're in trouble," Peter said, good-humoredly. "I told you to move here, but you wouldn't. You said you couldn't leave the city. And now look what's happened, trouble."

"Peter, you know who I got your number from. You're also in touch with the city. Even more so: sometimes you even design it."

"It's not reality for me," said Peter lightheartedly. "It's only on paper. It's like an author writing about murder. I'm interested in the city as a problem, as a tissue that doesn't belong to me. I don't have to be a murderer myself. Or the victim. It's even better this way. Who operates on his own leg?"

I couldn't listen to this.

"Peter, you don't understand. Diana . . . I don't know if you know what's going on with her."

"I know, I know," Peter chuckled. "She calls me often, too. She has her own problems. She also decided to move back to the city. She says that not enough blood flows through her here. That's why she left. When she left she said: I'll be at Roman's. You see, everything fits."

She calls him, I thought. Often. That explains the phone bill. It all fits.

"Peter, you have to help me. In the end, she is your wife."

"But how can I help you?" Peter was surprised. "You're there. I'm here. How shall I put it—there's an awful lot in between. We're not on the same ground."

"Peter," I said, "Peter, let's be reasonable."

"I'm being reasonable. You aren't. I'm doing fine. I'm not in trouble. I'm sitting here listening to the sound of one hand clapping."

"Oh, come on, Peter," I said. "What one hand clapping? You have a PC. You have a phone. Electricity. It's not what you moved into. You have more civilization in your house than I do. I didn't even buy a CD player. And you know how much I care about music."

"The computer's because of God," said Peter. "God needs a lot of space. I'm constantly buying new hard drives. And everything else. I even had electricity installed. For that I need money. And a telephone. It's all connected. That's why I draw plans. It's not about me. It's about Him. He's growing. It's lucky I have enough space."

"Don't they say there's only one God?" I asked.

"Of course there is, but his names are almost countless. The more names you give him, the easier it is to talk to him. The names are pieces which lead to the whole."

"Like grains of sand in a desert," I added, not without irony.

"Yes," Peter said calmly.

I thought about hanging up.

"And besides," he added, "there's a solution for everything. Also for you."

"I don't understand what you mean," I said. "What solution?"

"Leave the job," he suggested simply. "Sell the apartment. Write to your women that you're leaving, and don't say where. Throw away the pills. And come here. There's enough room. I have computer equipment in some of the rooms, but there are others."

Strangely, I found his proposal reasonable enough. After all, I'd get rid of a whole lot of troubles this way.

"And what would I do?" I asked.

"You'd enter the names in the computer. I need help. I sometimes get cramps in my fingers."

"What about Diana?" I said.

"Diana? Diana is just one of God's names, which are almost countless. And she thinks that for me she could be all the other names as well, just because she's my wife. But she's merely a piece in the whole. A piece called my wife."

Oh, yes, I thought, your wife. She calls me on my phone, eats my food, destroys my records. Sleeps in my bed. And although I would rather not tell you this, she sometimes sleeps in my bed even when I am there. To you she may be merely a piece, a grain of sand, but to me, let's face it, she's more like a whole. Piling on top of and bury-ing me.

"But . . . Peter, she's not all right. She gets up at night, sits by the window and looks at the street. Peter, there's nothing in our street at night. Nothing. And besides that, she's scratched some of my most precious records. She drags her nails over them, as if it didn't matter." (As if it were my skin, I thought.) "I can't just leave her alone." No, I can't, I thought.

"That's exactly what I'm saying, Roman," said Peter slowly. "In the city everything's different. I know. I was there. And not only that: I make towns. She didn't use to do all that here."

"You don't have a record player," I blurted.

"You and your record collection. I'm trying to make you see that the town is corroding her. It does that to everyone. It also corroded you. Get away if you can."

"But I don't have anything to do there. You have to understand me, Peter. I have a job here. I mean, I can get a job only here. I have friends here. I have . . ."

I was going to mention women, but I chose to clench my teeth and hold my tongue.

"You're not listening to me," said Peter calmly. "You're not listening at all. I'm trying to tell you a very simple thing, but you won't see: you can be happy."

I hung up.

That night I came home late. Rather late, I'd say. The streets seemed narrower than normal. They grew up clos-er, I thought. If you walk along them, it's like cutting into living flesh. You have to have power, the same power required for a stab with a knife. This is the city. Here one lives with the greediness of turbines. The city pulsates like a thousand-ton heart, filled with blood. Yes, that's why Diana looks at the streets at night. She studies the capillar-ies of a body that isn't hers. Not yet. In the sidewalk I recognized a harsh emotion which told me not to look at the ground, to avoid the ground.

"Your husband is listing all of God's names," I shouted to Diana from the door, when I finally found my way home. "And that's how he'll crawl under God's skin. And then he'll strike you with lightning because you're cheating on him. And there's more: he's going to build cities, new cities, and you'll be able to look at their streets all nights. And not only that. He's going to do it instead of me."

Diana looked at me with wonder.

"You who know everything and understand everything, did you know that too? He's going to get my place, and I his wife," I blathered on. "And neither of us wants what he's getting because of the thing itself. There's always something else behind it. He's going to take the town so that he has space for God with an almost infinite number of names. And I . . ."

I fell silent.

"Tell me," said Diana.

There's nothing to tell, I thought. The very last person I could explain this to is her. But where, then, is everybody else?

"Are you saying you don't want me?" said Diana and looked at me with devotion. "That I'm a burden to you? That I should go?"

Strange, I thought, why don't I say that that's how it is? Why don't I grab the opportunity, the first one I've had, and tell her that that's how it is and that she should get lost? And live as I lived before. And if I can't do this, because I can't bear those sad eyes, I could still say that that's not how it is, but, unfortunately, the circumstances . . . You're a married woman, I'd tell her, and I'm gay, and I have a steady partner—my boss—and now he suspects something, he's awfully jealous, he's firing me, understand me, this has got to end, I knew you'd understand, we'll always stay friends, if you need anything just call me, this was the best time of my life, and so on.

This way? Yes, it might work this way. It could. A possibility. But only one of many. Not the only one. And I've used this one before. Many times before.

"No," I said. "Don't go. I don't want to be alone. Talk to me."

"What shall I talk about?" asked Diana, bewildered. "I don't know what to talk about."

She doesn't know, I thought, finally there's something she does not know. This is good. Very good. If we start, we'll start from the same footing.

I stretched out on the floor. I laid my cheek on the nap of the mountain goat and noticed my head was resting on the red wine stain. What was the name of the woman I had thrown that party for? I thought for a moment. I couldn't remember, I remembered only the name of the man she had left with.

"Talk," I said. "About anything. Talk."

"I don't have anything to say," said Diana, and it seemed that she was about to cry. This is good, I thought. Very good.

I looked at her face, frightened, naked. Without make-up. Yes, I thought, she can stay here. After all, and considering everything else, she has nowhere else to go.

"Tell me something about . . . makeup. Tell me about it. What you call the different kinds, what they're like. I don't know anything about that."

"Me either," said Diana quietly. "Nothing. I was just practicing. Trying. Secretly. Everything that a woman should know about herself. It didn't work. You know. I'll never know how to live in the city. I should've known that before coming."

"One doesn't have to know everything. Sometimes, one can lie. If you lie to me I won't notice."

Diana nodded and sat on the floor. She placed my head in her lap.

"And there's something else before you begin," I said to her.

She looked at me questioningly.

"Put on a record," I said. "ABC: *4ever2gether.* It's right at the beginning. I have them arranged in alphabetical order." It's just kitschy enough, I thought. I always wanted to do something really kitschy, but I never dared. The boss had refined tastes. He would have thrown me out. And that was dismaying.

She didn't move.

"What are you waiting for?" I said.

"You told me to put on a record. Me?" she asked.

"You," I said. "Who else? There's just the two of us. Who else?"

I heard her nails slide over the grooves. It was a strange, unfamiliar sound. And, curiously, not unpleasant. Merely unfamiliar. Something that would take some getting used to. Like not rushing to work in the morning. Like not traveling this year, but using my savings to get us through until I found a new job. Like telling her, when she gets out of bed at night and goes to the window, to come back because there isn't anything out there that she needs. Like the fact that she'll want, if she's in the city and if she's a woman, to use makeup, and that it probably won't suit her. Like scratches on the back.

■ ☐ ■ ☐ ■

POSSIBILITY

AND THEN, SHE SAYS, THERE'S ALWAYS THE POSSIBILITY that our conclusions were all wrong. That we were, all along, working from the wrong convictions, that we imagined things wrongly: what we thought was the beginning of the story was actually its end.

Yes, he says, that's possible. Of course, it's possible.

Then they are silent for a long time.

■ □ ■ □ ■

ACTUALLY

I'D REALLY LIKE TO KNOW, SHE SAYS JUST AS I AM PUTTING these words down, why you prefer staring at the computer screen to going out with me to visit our friends. They've been inviting us for weeks, while you . . . First you don't feel like it, then you have a headache, then you have to figure something out, and then again you have some work that needs to be done right away, it's either one thing or another, the only thing you never do is take me out. Sometimes I think you're trying to cut me off from everyone, that maybe you want to have me all to yourself.

Maybe, I say, without looking at her. Maybe I do.

My bland admission surprises her. She is silent for a moment. Besides that, you'll ruin your eyes with the artificial light, she then says.

That's probably true, I say. And write. I must not let a single word escape me.

Maybe, she says slightly more quietly, it's because you know it's easier to stare at the screen than to look people in the eye. Maybe that's why you prefer staying at home and don't even want to do the shopping anymore.

Maybe that's why, I say, my fingers racing over the keyboard. Could you speak a bit slower, please?

Can't you keep up with me? she asks.

Hardly, I say. I'm really having difficulty.

It's probably a lot that you're listening to me at all, she says.

I write: It's probably a lot— Then I stop. I cease writing.

Listen, I say. Listen: I love you.

I know, she says. I know that.

I wait. I have no words left. I do not know what to say. I do not know what to write.

Love's not enough, she says.

It isn't? I ask. It probably really isn't, I think.

No. It isn't. There are also countless . . . other things.

What other things? I ask. I know: I'm just stalling, and stalling will get me nowhere. But what else could I do? I say to myself.

You don't expect me to spell them out for you, she says. I write: You don't expect me . . . I am tempted to add: they can't be expressed in words. It sounds so good that I can almost hear them as the next words she will utter. I wait for her to say them, but she does not. Quite the opposite: she is silent. And I do not add anything. A pity, I think, a real pity.

You should know them yourself, she says. Aren't you—

Don't tell me, I say. Don't tell me what I am.

But you are what you are, she argues, whether I say it or not.

Actually, I say, and realize with horror that I am about to start a long monologue, actually I never imagined I'd become what I finally did, I never imagined I'd spend most of my time closed up in my room, alone with myself, and that everything would be left up to me, that in this room I'd be making decisions about everything. Actually, I've always wanted to be a part of something larger than just myself, something whose limitations and significance I could never understand entirely, and something that would tell me what to do next. I always thought I'd be part of some vanguard group, that I'd know what to do, that I'd put together anew what was already known in such a way that it looked new, some-how as if I signed my work as Throbbing Gristle or the Test Department, my task would be clear and I wouldn't be looking for it alone, as, I admit, I'm doing now . . .

And why didn't you ever become something like that? she interrupts.

Yes, I whisper, why didn't I?

Actually, she continues, that means you lost.

Yes, I nod, actually I lost.

Actually, she says, everybody always ends up losing.

Wait, I disagree, that means . . .

No? she asks me. Don't they?

I don't know, I say barely audibly.

No? she insists. Don't they? Well, say it! Don't they? No?

What am I supposed to say? I ask. I've got nothing to say. I don't know.

Aha, she says, you don't know.

I don't know, I say. And think: I really don't know. At first I hesitate and then decide: no, I'm not going to write this down.

When I first met you, she says, I thought you knew everything, it seemed like there wasn't a single thing you didn't know about.

Is that so? I ask. I think: what made her think that? And about me, of all people. Strange, really strange.

You could've asked me, I would've told you I wasn't like that, I say to her. I would've told you that you were wrong.

Yes, I was wrong, she says.

True, she was wrong, so what's so special about that,

we all make mistakes, always and all the time, it's just that the lucky ones never realize it. But I won't tell her about that, I decide.

You were probably wrong about me, too, she says.

I consider her words. What do you mean? I ask.

Well, she says slowly, you thought I was different from what I am in reality.

In reality? I think. In reality?

You thought for instance I could handle money better. That you wouldn't have to take all kinds of jobs just to earn some money.

No, I say, I didn't think that.

You thought, she continues, I could cook better. That you wouldn't always have to add salt to the potatoes, and vinegar to the salad, and study cookbooks for recipes.

No, I say, now more quietly, I didn't think that.

You thought, she continues, I'd know what to do when the faucet breaks, or when the carpet starts to shred, and that you wouldn't have to deal with that.

No, I whisper, I didn't think that.

You thought, she says finally, that you'd be left in peace to sit in front of the screen and do your work, while I'd take care of everything else. That's what you thought.

I do not say anything. I remain silent.

But, she says, I don't know how to do all those things. We've been together long enough for you to know this by now, even if you did hope in the beginning that things would turn out differently.

Yes, I think, that's true. That's it, hope.

It was an empty hope, she says.

Automatically, I move. I bend toward the keyboard.

Don't do that, she says.

What? I ask.

Don't put my words down. Then they're no longer mine, and I don't want that.

I don't put your words down, I say, surprised.

But you do. At night, when you fall asleep I get up, switch on the computer, and read what you've written during the day. And everything the women in your stories say are my words. And what the men say are your words.

That's not true, I say. Nothing I write is real. It's all fiction.

Then you're also fiction, she says. And me too.

I consider her words: yes, it's possible. True, it's possible. I'll have to think about that, I say to myself. And then I suddenly realize: what am I thinking about?

I, she says, I . . .

Yes, I say.

I don't want to be fiction.

Her words sound somehow hollow. I am not tempted to write them down at all.

I'd like to live, really live.

This reminds me of a myriad of things I have heard before. A really worn-out phrase. If I write it down, I will have to twist it somehow, make it ironic in some way. But how do I do that?

Aren't you living now? I ask. If she says: Do you call this living? we're lost deep in melodrama, and not even original at that, I think to myself.

Now? she asks.

The moment of decision is prolonged.

I'm living now as well, she says, but not the way I'd like to.

The circle is closing, I think.

Actually, I say, that means you lost as well.

Actually, she says, everybody always ends up losing.

The circle's closed, I think. I look at the screen. On it there are glittering words I do not understand, words that mean nothing to me. I switch the computer off without saving the file on the floppy disc.

Listen, I say, this is pointless.

Maybe it really is, she admits without hesitation. So what do you suggest? Probably nothing.

It's true, she's right, I say to myself. Nothing. I've got nothing to suggest.

Am I right? she says.

Right, I affirm.

So everything will go on like before, she states.

Now I am somewhat puzzled. Like before? I say. I thought you'd—

Me? she says.

You.

I would what?

Well, that you'd change it. That you'd probably go.

Go where? To our friends? To visit them?

No. Not to our friends. That you'd leave forever.

Forever, I think, that's a strong word.

I have nowhere to go, she says calmly.

I think about this carefully: she really doesn't have anywhere to go. It's difficult knowing that, I think.

You're everything I have, she says, and I don't even have you.

You know, I say, it's not important to have. It's important to be.

I listen to my voice: it sounds thin, and papery.

To be? she asks.

To know that you are, that you exist, I say. And I listen to my papery voice. The rest comes out later, gradually, almost unnoticed. The rest comes.

I've known that I am for a long time. For a very long time, she says under her breath.

And? I say. And think: now she's making up her mind.

Nothing, she says. The rest hasn't come yet. And maybe it never will come. But let's drop the subject. There's no need to complicate matters. Actually, the thing is very simple. I find life—

She halts.

I wait. She, however, maintains the silence. She finds it—, I say to myself. What? I wonder. Difficult? A burden? Nice? Strange? Necessary?

I look at her: she's looking through the window. For a moment I am tempted to go see what is on the other side of the windowpane. Is there anything? Maybe, it occurs to me, she's just looking at her own reflection, with the features standing out increasingly clearly in the dusk. Maybe, I say to myself, she's waiting for it to get dark, and then all her images will become one.

What are you looking at? I ask.

Actually, she says very quietly, so that I have to bend forward and listen intently, actually at nothing.

I step over to where she is standing. She is right: there is actually nothing to be seen from there. I look and look, and see nothing. So, I say to myself, that's it, then. There is nothing. Not even a reflection in the glass.

We see the same thing, I think, so we are made of the same stuff after all, so we do belong together. And for this reason I won't turn the computer on again, I won't bend over the keyboard, I'll get dressed and go out, we'll visit our friends together, and maybe at least today she'll think that it has come, the rest, the thing we've been waiting for. Actually, that's what I have to do. I must. That's why we'll get dressed, we'll go out, we'll ring our friends' doorbell, we'll drink what they offer, we'll talk about whatever the conversation is, and I'll look them in the eye. Tonight I actually have to.

■ □ ■ □ ■

DAMP WALLS

IN MY ROOM. IN MY BED. THAT'S JUST NOT ACCEPTABLE.

The sound of the running water dies down. Hand me a towel, please, she says. We can't talk like this: me naked, you in gray tweed.

I want to say: come on! I want to say: now listen to me! I don't say anything. I mumble: towel? I watch a rivulet slither down her breast, a small drop that gets smaller, and disappears. Will it still drop? I think.

Yes, the towel. Behind you. Turn around. That one, the pink one.

I swallow. Pink, like the nipples of her breasts. I feel softness in my palm. I let go.

So, she says, with her shoulders peeking over the cotton barrier. What was it you wanted to discuss?

In my room, I say. In my bed.

This isn't going to work, I think. That's the way I started, and then she wanted a towel. Differently, I'll have to tackle it differently.

I watch: winding streams on the tiles. Capillaries. I feel the pulse in my temples, on my forehead, in my neck. I know: something must be done. I know: something has to be said.

Please, I say, why don't you dry off when you get out of the tub? What's a towel for, anyway?

My voice, firm and self-confident. Richard Burton starring as Tito.

I watch her: does it seem that way to her too?

She looks at me. I wait: what will she say? How will she defend herself?

The towel? she says. It falls to her feet.

I know I'm perspiring. If she notices, I've lost.

Don't be evasive, I say. I try hard not to look away.

You know, I say. In my room. In my bed.

Oh, that, she says. That's Donald.

Donald? I ask.

Yes, Donald.

But what's he doing there? He's stark naked. Smoking a cigar. Imported. Scattering the ashes on the sheets.

She watches me. I wait: Will she say anything? Is she going to defend herself?

Yesterday, at dinner, she says, I read you that newspaper article, but you didn't listen. I read to you. About that research in the U.S. About women my age. In the West, every successful woman my age has steady relationships with at least two men.

You read to me? I say.

At dinner. Don't you remember? Fried hot dogs with cheese?

I can remember the meal, I say, but . . . I pause.

I'm listening, she says.

But he's black.

We're not in Pretoria, she says.

We're not exactly in the West either, I say.

We aren't? she asks.

I know: now we're going too far. That's not what I wanted to talk about.

He, I say. Why is he here?

For me, she says. Because of that American research.

I watch: her feet have been swallowed by the pink coil.

Pick up the towel, I say.

Pick it up yourself.

I swallow. Because of the American research? I say.

Yes, you know, about successful women.

I swallow.

And you . . . He?

She nods. Don't take it personally. I just had to find another one, you understand. I've got nothing against you. It's just mathematics.

What mathematics, I object, when he's in my room, in my bed, and smoking foreign cigars?

Mathematics. You and him, that makes two. And, so . . .

Are you saying . . . A steady relationship? A successful woman?

Of course. I knew you'd understand. It's nothing personal.

I bend down. She bends down as well. She picks up the towel. I think: now she'll wrap herself again. Then I'll be able to let her have it. Then I'll be able to.

She doesn't wrap herself in the towel.

I rub my hand against the tiles. They're damp.

How long has this been going on? I ask.

Since today, she says. She folds the towel and puts it on the shelf above the sink.

So as of today, I think, she's a successful woman with a steady relationship with two men. And yet she folds a wet towel. Well, well.

Are you going to get dressed? I say.

She stares at me.

Aren't you going to get undressed? she says.

I watch her.

But, I hear myself say, what about Donald?

Donald will wait, she replies. He's one of two. He has to learn how to wait. To be patient.

Yes, I say, he has to learn.

So then, she says, what are you waiting for?

Yes, I whisper, what am I waiting for?

She takes a step toward me. I avert my eyes. And I see the mirror. My face, covered with vapor.

Wait, I say, I can't do that. He's in my room, in my bed . . . He'll hear us.

Let him hear, she says. Let him learn who's the boss.

I retreat: to the wall, close to the wall. Press against it. I can feel the moisture seep through my jacket, trickle down my back.

The walls are damp, I say. You should . . .

Yes, damp, she says.

I fall silent.

Take off your clothes, she says. We can't do it like this: me naked, you in gray tweed.

And so: inside me, persistent rivulets gurgle, while in my room, in my bed, a black man, Donald, smokes a cigar. I'm here, trapped between damp walls, I say to myself. If I talk, it will last. If I say nothing, it will pass. I have a choice. That's what's important: choice. So then? So then.

■ □ ■ □ ■

BILLIE HOLIDAY

WHAT IF, SHE SAYS, WE PLAYED THAT OLD BILLIE HOLIDAY record? Would you kiss me then?

You don't have it anymore, he says. You don't have that record anymore.

How do you know? she asks. There are some things one never loses.

But not that record, he says. Do you remember how we searched for it last year? That time we went to the cinema and were both very sad afterward, and we got drunk and looked for that record and it wasn't anywhere, and we just danced, without music. Don't you remember?

Yes, I remember, she says. But we got drunk that time and we didn't look everywhere. The record could have still been someplace, it's just that we didn't find it that time.

And you found it afterward? he asks. You?

I do the cleaning in this apartment, in case you've already forgotten, she says quietly. I'm the one who goes rummaging through the closets.

And now you have it? Do you have it? he asks, a trifle impatiently.

It doesn't matter, she says quietly. I don't think it matters.

No? he says. You don't?

You didn't answer my question, she says. You didn't tell me.

What? he says.

Well, she says, if you'd kiss me.

If I had the record.

What does that mean—if I had?

It's mine, isn't it? You bought it for me, for my birthday. Don't you remember?

He remains silent.

Yes, I remember, he says slowly. Yes, that's right.

There's also writing on it, she says. It says: to you, the one and only. And your name is on it. And the date.

Is it? he says.

Yes. Don't you remember?

I remember, he says, quite slowly, not sounding very convinced.

You've forgotten, she says, you've forgotten. To you, the one and only. You forgot everything. And you wouldn't even kiss me anymore. Not even if I played that record. Because you think it's too late. Don't you?

What? he says.

Don't be evasive, she says. You know what I'm talking about. That's what you think, isn't it?

He says nothing. When he finally breaks the silence, his voice is hoarse and it breaks against the walls of the room.

Wouldn't it be better, he says, if people solved things like this in some other way? Differently?

In what way? she asks. How differently?

With less . . . pain. More easily.

And how do you imagine that? she says slowly.

Let's say: write about it to the papers. And then people would respond. Give advice. They would say: it happened to me too, and then . . .

Dear Abby?

Dear Abby.

And how would this help? Advice? We've had more than enough advice, everybody told us their story, everyone has one. And it was no use.

Even if it was no use, he says. It would be there. It's easier if you know you're not the only one it's happened to.

You mean like you said the other day: that it's necessary to distribute the pain equally? she asks. That everyone gets an equal share of it? And that this way it's easier for everyone?

Yes, he nods seriously. That's it.

Interesting, she says. Interesting.

What? he asks. What's interesting?

She opens her mouth, and he, against his will, notices how this mouth is smaller than the one he remembers. Something is missing, he thinks. No, not missing—it has grown smaller.

The telephone rings.

The phone's ringing, she says.

I can hear it, he says, it's ringing. And now what?

Answer it. Pick it up. It's for you, I'm sure.

What if it isn't? Maybe it's for you.

It's never for me, she says. Nobody ever calls me. It is for you.

He picks up the receiver. Hello? he says. Oh, it's you, he says then. How are you?

While the voice at the other end of the line is answering, he covers the receiver with his palm and whispers: You were right. It really is for me.

It's her, isn't it? she says.

It's her, he nods seriously, and then immediately says into the receiver: Oh, yeah? Is that so? Really?

She turns and leaves the room. He keeps glancing at her, while speaking smoothly into the telephone: Mhm. Yes. You don't say!

Music is heard from the adjoining room. He frowns and says into the telephone: What?

She returns, leans against the wall and looks at him. The corners of her mouth curve, and then drop again. And a few more times like that.

He says into the telephone: This? Billie Holiday.

She nods. Yes, Billie Holiday, she says quietly.

He says: Old, of course it's old.

She steps close to him and puts her arms around his waist.

He says: I like it.

She leans her head against his belly.

He says: What? No, I'm not alone.

She gives him a strong hug.

He says: She's here. Near me.

She draws his shirt out of his trousers.

He says: What do you mean, how near? Yes, she's in this room. Yes, close enough to touch.

She draws her palm across his skin.

He says, somewhat reluctantly: I don't know. He covers the receiver and mouths a question.

She says, loudly, as if they were alone: What?

He keeps covering the receiver, and whispers: She's asking if you mind my talking to her.

I do mind, she says calmly. And continues to caress his skin.

He removes his hand from the receiver and wipes the sweat from his forehead. She doesn't mind, he says unconvincingly into the telephone.

Did she fall for it? she asks.

He nervously covers the receiver with his hand.

What? he says. No, that's music. Billie Holiday.

She rises, steps close to him, and kisses him on the mouth.

He takes hold of her chin and turns her face away, but not with much conviction.

Of course I love you, he says into the receiver.

Tell her you're lying, she says quietly. Tell her.

Really, he says. I do.

You know you love me, she says with determination.

Me. Although you don't show it. Although you think you shouldn't show it.

He lets the hand holding the receiver dangle at his hip. How do you know? he says.

Your skin tells me, she says calmly. At night, when we're lying together, in the same bed, your skin tells me: I love you.

How's that? he says. My skin?

Skin talks, she says with conviction. Didn't you know?

No, I didn't, he admits.

There's a lot more you don't know, it seems to me, she says, somehow compassionately.

He looks at her for a while, then drops his eyes and notices the receiver in his hand. What did you say? he says. And waits.

Then he hangs up.

She's no longer there, he says.

That's the way it should be, she says. She hung up. She knew you were lying. Like I know.

No, he objects, I'm not lying.

The skin, she says. Your skin gives you away.

My skin? he says and draws his palm across his cheek. What's all this about skin?

Yeah, what about it? she asks. Why don't you listen to it anymore? Why don't you follow it? Why do you want to get out of it?

Listen? Follow? Out? he asks. Hey, listen, what's your game? What are you trying to tell me?

That you don't know how to listen, she says calmly. And that's why you think that all things come to an end. That they pass away and are gone. That they disappear without a trace. While in reality they're still there, only different. If you listened, you'd know.

I don't understand, he says.

You don't understand because you don't listen, she

says. Everything lasts. It's true that it sometimes isn't the way it used to be, it's true that it sometimes looks old and out of style. But it lasts. Just a sort of film covers it. And everything is the same as it used to be. The same beautiful things. Just a little . . . older. And that's why they look strange to you.

Like Billie Holiday? he says. Beautiful, but old. And that's why it crackles.

That's right. Like Billie Holiday.

But we lost it, he says to himself.

And found it again, she says.

You found it, he says. You. I . . . I'm just listening. From a distance.

Once you said, she says, that everything looked beautiful that way. From a distance. Because you could imagine it your way.

Once, he says, once I had all the answers. I knew everything. What. Why. How.

And now it's over, she says. You don't have any answers anymore. But you still have something. Something more.

What? he asks.

Me, she says. You've got me.

I can't, he says. You know it doesn't work that way.

What way? she asks.

You're not enough. I have to eat. I have to sleep, I have to . . .

What? she says. What else? Tell me.

What else am I supposed to say? he says.

Her, she says. You haven't mentioned her.

Why does it always end with her? he says, bad-tempered. Why does everything lead to her in the end?

Yes, why? she says thoughtfully. Why, when in reality . . .

The music stops.

What is it? he starts. Is it the end of the record?

Wait, she says. There's more.

And really, in the next room Billie Holiday starts singing again.

The sky was blue
And high above
The moon was new
And so was love . . .

That's what you sang to me when we were at the seaside, he grows tender.

No, no, she says.

Yes, he continues. Quite a while ago. When we walked along the beach in the evening, and you told me which star was which. I was absolutely enchanted; I don't know anything about stars.

No, no, she persists.

Yes, nothing. And then we sat down somewhere by the sea. It looked like the middle of nowhere, remember? And we drank all the fruit brandy we could get into that little flask you gave me when you were selling them at the Christmas fair. And you held my hand a little longer every time I handed you the drink.

That wasn't me, she says with determination.

No? he says incredulously.

No.

That's right. He grows pensive. Her skin was cooler than yours.

Was it?

Yes. Cool and smooth.

And mine isn't?

I know every pore on your skin.

Pore? she says.

Crease and scratch, he says, somewhat impatiently.

And that's why you don't want it anymore, she says calmly. Are there many?

I don't know, he says. But I know them all.

They do no harm, she says. It's like Billie Holiday's records. Scratches belong there. Without them it would be something different.

That's just it, he says.

It — what?

It — something different.

So that's what it's all about, she says. You're fed up. And you think it'll take your mind off it, if it's something different. And that you won't notice that it's sometimes the same as it was before. Because you're the same. It's the same, except for the scratches that come after a long time.

No, he says. What are you talking about? That's non-sense.

Nonsense, she nods. As always. The same, I tell you.

The telephone rings again.

Let it ring, she says. It'll stop.

Aren't you interested in who it is? he asks. It might be for you.

I know who it is, she says. It's not for me.

If it isn't for you, he says, then it's for me. And if it's for me, I really don't see why I shouldn't answer it.

Because you don't have time, she says.

I don't have time? What am I doing that is so impor-tant that I don't have time?

You're listening to Billie Holiday.

I think I can listen to Billie Holiday and talk on the phone. Both at the same time. I think I can manage that.

No, you can't. Not if you listen to Billie Holiday and kiss me at the same time. Then you can't talk on the phone.

Listen to Billie Holiday and kiss you? Like in the old times?

That's right. Only with more scratches. With the coat-ing. With everything that came along. And so, differently.

But look, the phone won't stop ringing. It just keeps

ringing. I can't listen to Billie Holiday with the phone ringing all the time. I can't kiss you if it's ringing, and it's for me, and I know who it is.

Well, then answer and tell her, she says. Tell her what you're doing. And it'll stop ringing. And it'll be easier.

He looks at her. He looks at the telephone. He looks at his hand hovering over the receiver.

I should tell her? Really? And if I do tell her—what'll happen then? Will it be any different? Changed in any way?

Tell her. There are things that don't seem to exist unless you say them. Maybe this one isn't that kind . . . But then, maybe it is. Tell her, and we'll see what happens next.

He picks up the receiver. He looks at her again, and she nods. He also lifts his head and bends it upon his chest in a slow arc. Singing is still heard from the background. The record is crackling slightly.

I can't, he says into the receiver held in his outstretched arm, far away from his mouth. I can't. I'm listening to Billie Holiday. Still. In the same way. But differently. Do you hear? Do you understand?

■ □ ■ □ ■

HODALYI

THE WOMAN GROANED. NOT NOW, HE THOUGHT. THERE was a flash. The sirens screamed. He rolled off her. The windowpane hummed. He pulled on his pants. Somebody clattered down the stairs. He looked through the window. People raced about in all directions. He threw his jacket over his arm. He walked toward the door. The woman hid her face in her hands. Airplane engines droned. He stopped at the door. The woman looked at him. She opened her mouth. There was an explosion, somewhere nearby. He turned around and ran. He sailed down the stairs. He was in the hall. A machine gun rattled. Somebody called his name. He spun around. It was dark. There were several of them. They were hiding below the staircase. Then he saw they were children. Kids from the neighborhood. They were always pestering him. They wanted money, but he never had any. It's going to be about money again, he thought. He waited. The oldest one peeled himself from the dark. The one called Gorgo. He was thirteen years old. "We're going to kill you, Hodalyi," he said in a hoarse voice. "Why do you keep coming here? We're going to kill you." He waved them off. He had no time for their games. He turned. Upstairs, a door opened. A shadow fell along the staircase. Somebody was watching what was going on. He dashed out into the street. He wasn't even through the door when it hit him. A sweet taste spread through his mouth. Puzzled, he watched the pool of blood on the pavement grow closer, closer. He groaned. Not now, he thought.

■ □ ■ □ ■

TEMPORARY RESIDENCE

for L. A.

IT IS HUMID. A MAN AND A WOMAN ARE LYING ON THE bed. The fan slices the air with regular strokes. He is wearing striped boxer shorts, fraying at the edges. She is covered with a soiled sheet, spattered with humid patches. The man stretches his arm into the air. Beads of sweat glide along it.

The woman says: Why this room? Why are we here? You said: temporarily. You can dance. You can sing. You've got money. Everybody loves you. You always know what to say. And when to say it. You can go wherever you want to. Why did you lock the door? There are no more wars. We can leave. Maybe they're selling flowers again outside. Probably plastic, but that's all right as well. That way you don't buy too many at a time. Let's go. Let's go. Buy me flowers. And then we'll go for an ice cream. The taste remains the same. The one.

The man doesn't answer. He looks at nothing. The fan slices the air with regular strokes. A radio hums somewhere. No distinguishable sound.

Something tells me the dead will rise again, says the woman. But I'm not afraid, we'll chase them away, we know how to handle them. You have to know how, and then it's okay. If we pretend nothing's happened, they'll go away by themselves. And I'm not scared of the living anymore. They're not as terrible as I first thought. And there are fewer of them. Far fewer than I thought.

The man doesn't answer. He is watching the bead glide down his arm. He purses his lips and blows. The bead stops for a moment. Then the man presses his lips together and the bead continues gliding.

And if I look toward the sky, the world appears smaller now, says the woman. And the stars closer. It's not the way it used to be before. Nothing. Nothing. True, I've also sometimes said: everything should be changed. But if you change everything from beginning to end, in the end it's your turn. And who knows for certain what happens? I'm telling you, this is dangerous. I'd rather have it the way it was before, when it changed by itself. But, if it isn't . . .

The man remains silent, looks at the ceiling. He stretches his arm into the air. Beads of sweat drop onto his face. The radio static increases.

And the woman says: It isn't good if things change. For instance: I loved you better when you didn't have anything. And then it changed. Of course I still love you. But it's the little things that have changed. Now I don't love your mouth anymore. I don't love your eyes anymore. I don't love the color of your sweaters anymore. I don't love the way you hold a pencil anymore. Your mouth. Your eyes. The color of your sweaters. The way you hold a pencil. I don't love any of those things anymore. No more. The little things. It's not good if they change.

The man doesn't answer. The fan slices the air with regular strokes. Rain begins to patter against the window.

And the woman says: Take my language. It isn't mine anymore. They put all the words into my mouth. And I have only them. Plenty of them. I can't get rid of them, no matter how hard I try. They're just here, inside. And you won't take me out. No. We've been in this room for an eternity. You don't say anything. You listen to the radio, but there's never any music. If there was, we could dance. But you wouldn't want to. No, you don't want to anymore. You feel fine here. I listen too, but they don't say anything. I learn about everything from the whispers whirling around inside my head. And they don't want out. No, they don't want to get out at all. Maybe it's like this only in this room, but you won't give me the key. Perhaps you don't have it at all. I'm tired of this room. You said: temporarily. I don't know if you've noticed, but this has been going on for a while. Going on for as long as I can remember. And we eat nothing but canned food. It's bad for me. I can feel my skin going. I don't know if new skin will grow in its place. And even if it does: my old skin was good. And the radio . . . The radio doesn't talk anymore. They don't play any music either. I don't know if you've noticed. I don't know if this means anything. But there isn't any music. There isn't. Just that crackling noise. Which never stops. And this canned food. No, I don't want it. I want some ice cream. And flowers.

The man doesn't answer. The fan slices the air with regular strokes. Traces of sweat meander down his outstretched arm.

Do you think it will ever end? asks the woman. I mean, whatever. That the fan will stop. That the radio will stop crackling. Yes, I'd really like that. That the tins will run out. I'd like that too, but I don't know if we have anything else. And I want the heat to die down. Do you think it will end? You said: temporarily. What do you think now?

The man doesn't answer. The fan slices the air with regular strokes.

■ □ ■ □ ■

RAI

THE MAN DOES NOT HAVE ANY LUGGAGE, YET IT SEEMS HE is beginning a journey, or perhaps ending one. He is alone on the first morning bus that leaves the suburb; it has not yet dawned, the driver is having difficulty fighting off his drowsiness, his head droops, nobody gets on at the stops, the town is asleep, it is cold, the man pushes his hands deep into his pockets, leans his forehead against the damp glass to clear his head.

The bus pulls in at a stop and the man slowly drags himself to the door. The driver turns, and the man raises his hand hello. The driver nods and reaches for the buttons: the door unfolds slowly and wind gushes into the vehicle; a few snowflakes have caught the current and they immediately melt in the warmth. The driver turns on the radio and the morning program blares, accordions and vocals. The man strokes his forehead, leaving a wet trace on his palm.

He gets off the bus, and straightens his coat. Snowflakes cling to him, slowly but relentlessly. He reaches into his pocket, puts on the earphones. The dry, caustic voice of Cheb Khaled trickles from the Walkman. Slow, tired steps outline a path in the snow. He knows where he is going, where he is coming from. In front of the house, from whose sidewalk the snow will have to be cleared. A turn of the key, a habitual and familiar gesture. Then the stairs: first floor. In the kitchen there will be the woman with swollen eyes, she will be clutching a sheet around herself, wrapped over her nightgown. On the table, a small puddle of coffee grounds. First she will look at him for a long time, and his eyes will smart at the sight of the salty traces below her eyelids. Then she will ask him why he didn't stay with the one he spent the night with. When he tells her that he spent the night walking through frosty forest, watching moonlight fight its way through treetops, all the while listening to Algerian rai, her lips will purse into a cold, offended line. You know, you can tell me the truth, she will say again, I can handle the truth better than these senseless lies. I understand, you love her more than me. But why do you keep coming back then, why don't you just stay there? And he will know again that there is no sense in objecting, in explaining. He will put his earphones on and the cassette will play again and again, while he is wiping the table, washing dishes, with the woman watching him, wrapped in her stained and patched sheet, motionless. And the drawling voice of Cheb Khaled will slow down, until the batteries finally give out.

WRITINGS FROM AN UNBOUND EUROPE

Words Are Something Else
DAVID ALBAHARI

Skinswaps
ANDREJ BLATNIK

My Family's Role in the World Revolution and Other Prose
BORA ĆOSIĆ

Peltse and Pentameron
VOLODYMYR DIBROVA

The Victory
HENRYK GRYNBERG

The Tango Player
CHRISTOPH HEIN

A Bohemian Youth
JOSEF HIRŠAL

Mocking Desire
DRAGO JANČAR

Balkan Blues: Writing Out of Yugoslavia
JOANNA LABON, ED.

The Loss
VLADIMIR MAKANIN

Compulsory Happiness
NORMAN MANEA

Zenobia
GELLU NAUM

Rudolf
MARIAN PANKOWSKI

The Houses of Belgrade
The Time of Miracles
BORISLAV PEKIĆ

Merry-Making in Old Russia and Other Stories
The Soul of a Patriot
EVGENY POPOV

Estonian Short Stories
KAJAR PRUUL AND DARLENE REDDAWAY, EDS.

Death and the Dervish
MEŠA SELIMOVIĆ

Fording the Stream of Consciousness
In the Jaws of Life and Other Stories
DUBRAVKA UGREŠIĆ